D1387121

CATHOLIC BOY

Rosemary Jenkinson

Doire Press

First published in 2018

Doire Press
Aille, Inverin
Co. Galway
www.doirepress.com

Layout & design: Lisa Frank

Printed by Clódóirí CL
Casla, Co. na Gaillimhe

ISBN 978-1-907682-60-5

We gratefully acknowledge the assistance of The Arts Council of Northern Ireland.

CONTENTS

One day in Berlin came a telegram: 'Found a wonderful green stone. Come immediately, Zorba.'

— Nikos Kazantzakis

REVIVAL

How could anyone forget him from the TV screen in the seventies and eighties, hunched, swift, stalking, surveying the greenbaize plain, his nostrils quivering, sensing he *had* his opponent. He was all lean muscle bristling under his suit, an edgy Belfast boy with barroom pallor and he'd strike—an explosive cue action, a punch winding the audience into tumultuous applause, the trademark whip through the air. He was Alex 'Hurricane' Higgins, two times snooker world champion and working-class hero. When he was on top, he'd strut, preeningly sexual, loose-limbed in the pleasure of predation, and clean up the table in seconds; then back to his seat where, confined and restless, he would light up yet another cigarette.

'What's your name?' asked the tiny, elderly man with the pinched face. He was wearing a raincoat and a hat. His glasses were teetering right on the tip of his nose in the same way that he was standing on the edge of the kerb.

'Cara. What's yours?'

I knew his name but I kept looking. He was so frail and drained of colour. The only thing that convinced me I was right was his blue eyes.

'Alex Higgins.' His voice was light but husky, the whisper of dried leaves spiralling on a pavement.

Pure fluke had brought me to the taxi rank outside Lavery's on the way home from the pub. I'd thought about trying the one up on Castle Street but, just as I'd arrived, two girls from East Belfast were being turned away.

'You won't take us, so you won't?' one girl was shouting angrily over her shoulder. 'Well, let me tell you this, our fathers built this city!'

'They built this city...' derided the taxi driver at the door, letting fly with a bombardment of cracking laughter. I walked on. I didn't want to pretend I was a West Belfast partisan just to get a taxi. That was the thing hard to stomach about Belfast, it was all black and white, East or West, with us or against us...

There was nothing black or white about Alex Higgins' accent. It was English barbed with Belfast, impossible to pin down, a changeable hybrid of the rhythms of middle-class society and backstreet banter.

'Have you been drinking in Lavery's?' I asked him.

Lavery's was infamous for its back bar which never seemed to release its clients before kicking-out time. A bit of a holding pen for hard-core alcoholic sorts.

'No. They barred me,' he said, smiling with some pride. 'I was in Sandy Row. They're all mad there.'

We were headed the same direction so we shared a taxi. We didn't live that far up the Lisburn Road but within five minutes he had established quite a lot about my life. He fired out questions sharper than I'd ever known anyone. Like a man in an incredible rush. He found out I was looking to move house and offered to rent me out the other room in his flat. He was often abroad, he said, he was planning to go for three months to Australia. I could see it now if I wanted to pop round for a drink.

I knew so many stories about Alex from around town, his begging, his shoplifting, his aggression. I knew I shouldn't be going to his flat but I was curious and he was perfectly compos mentis for all the drink; if he'd had the physique of Mike Tyson I might have thought twice.

The flat was pine-floored, fresh-painted and modern.

'It's a lovely flat.'

'This is the room,' he said, ushering me through. 'I call it the occidental room.'

The bed was covered in bags and suitcases and turfed-out clothes. The whole flat gave me an impression of someone just passing through. Half-submerged in the waves of fabric, as though washed up from the distant past, was a framed photograph of himself in his playboy heyday and Peter Stringfellow sitting smiling over a giant magnum of champagne that seemed dwarfed between them. He was telling me that the Snooker Association was going to pay the rent for him for life. It sounded generous but I couldn't help thinking they must have figured it wouldn't be for much longer.

He took me into the kitchen to get a drink. He didn't want one. He only drank Guinness now. He opened his fridge to reveal a bottle of white wine and a bottle of vodka chilling, icy-breathed. Otherwise there was only a mauled meat pie and a couple of eggs.

We sat down on the sofa and Alex flicked on the TV. On the coffee table lay his crumpled income support booklet and a large piece of cannabis resin, square like cue chalk.

He checked the racing results and tutted.

'I do the horses every day. Pick fourteen out of thirty-two. It's my system. Stick around and I'll show you.'

'But does it work?'

He grinned at the pertinence of my question and rewarded me with a tap of his hand on my head as though bestowing a blessing.

'Not often.'

He began rolling a joint, putting in a generous dose of hash. Suddenly he sprang up to have a look for something on the shelves and I noticed there was still that energy in his movements, reminiscent of his lethal progress round the snooker table, the rhythm born of a killer instinct. Without an outlet that instinct had by all accounts turned in on itself in a gradual, smothering suicide. And then I realised uncomfortably that tonight I was probably there as his prey, but it was a little late to worry about it.

He finally found the photograph he was looking for.

'Who's that?' he pointed.

'Steve Davis.'

'Very good.' He was impressed. 'I'll tell you about him. He was once seven frames up on me and I still beat him. After that, we all called him Seven-Up. And who's the one on the left?' he questioned in the way a father would expect his child to shout out, 'Daddy!'

'You.'

'When I had more hair,' he winked, stroking his head.

'I used to watch you on TV when I was a kid. You were the greatest player ever.'

He hadn't thought I was that old but his face lit up.

'That was when snooker was the game. We were the players.' His eyes lowered shyly, falling away under the downturn of his latter years. 'All the ones nowadays are little squirts. Look at that Mark Williams wandering round the table like a tramp. Can't be bothered even to shave. None of them have any presence. Practise eleven hours a day. I only practised seven, then I went boozing. I had showbiz in my veins. I could have played the guitar, instead I picked up a different piece of wood.'

'You can't play any more?'

'No. It's a long story,' he said uncertainly, scouring my face as though for some item hidden in the back-page columns. 'I haven't the strength now.'

I went ahead and mentioned I'd heard about the throat cancer though I wasn't sure I should. Alex wasn't fazed.

'Yeah. It's in remission but it's not gone. I can't swallow properly, means I can't eat. That's why I'm so thin. But I've packed in the fags for good now — I only ever smoke a spliff.'

I felt embarrassed, at an unfair advantage. I had insider information. To use Alex's racing terminology, I knew the form. He'd tried to beg a packet of twenty Regal off a friend of mine days after he'd claimed in *The Sunday World* that he'd given up smoking.

He lit up the joint and passed it across. 'Go on, keep it live.' I shook my head but he insisted, observing me smoke, almost monitoring the changes in me. He pulled my hand over.

'Look at the state of those nails. Why do you bite them?'

'Stress.'

'I know. I'm nervous too.'

I laughed because Alex didn't need to tell me. He was the nerviest player I'd ever seen. I had this in common with him: nerve endings that buzzed with a kind of internal tinnitus to the touch, an electrical storm within, and the fact was the ingestion of slow smoke helped, easing into the eye of the storm and spreading outwards in a calm, white fog.

His touch along the back of my fingers was light.

'Why don't you give me a massage instead of biting your nails... go on... you never know, it might titillate you.'

It flashed across my mind that I'd inadvertently got myself into *Sunday World* territory. All too clearly I could imagine the headline to our night of passion — 'Alex still has plenty of chalk in his cue!' Lascivious lines about tipping the velvet and sinking the pink also sprang to mind.

'You can live here no problem,' he was saying gently. 'You be good to me and I'll be good to you.'

I turned him down and he didn't seem bothered. The joint had kicked in and he sat slumped, wasted, a spent force, his lips moving like red rags fluttering on the heel of a gale. He began to cough, the rattle in the back of his throat like fireworks in the distance, a fusillade of tiny exploding stars.

He pointed up to a portrait of two blond children.

'Haven't seen them in fourteen years. My wife wouldn't let me...' he muttered with grievance and put his hand over his eyes as if looking into the past. 'I was world champion...' He was talking to himself now and I understood how he woke up unhappy every morning, raddled with cancer and memories and his own lies and the slough of self-pity. On the shelf stood an old silver trophy burnished like a bruise, a container now for junk.

He roused himself and reached out for my hand.

'Go on,' he urged. 'It was my birthday last week. I'm fifty-three and I haven't had it in ages. Stay. You can make yourself an egg in the morning before you go to work.'

'Much as that is tempting, Alex, I'm going to refuse,' I said, getting up. I saw myself out and his head half-turned above the top of the sofa to say, 'Fair enough.'

A week later I went to see Richard Dormer's one-man act, *Hurricane*, which was playing at the Old Museum Arts Centre. He was Alex personified, tiny and withered as now, and, as the young uninhibited, shotmaking genius, he blazed across the stage, twirling his cue like a band-pole on the glorious Twelfth, a spiralling centrifugal force out of control. He *was* Alex and through him we relived the rise, the fall, the revival, the marriage break-up, the boozing, the womanising, the bans and the irreversible decline, and our hearts willed him on to his famous, tear-filled victory, to that crowning moment to a life of passion when he beckoned desperately for his child, and we stood and applauded till the stage blackened and died.

Outside it was still light and the wind was strong and gusting as if generated by the energy summoned up in that small auditorium. All I could think about was Alex while the twitters, 'brilliant,' 'marvellous,' from the lips of people who would despise him now if they saw him, flew round the road and fractured into the merest of sounds.

I saw him once more, this time in the morning at the bus stop near my house.

'Hello, big girl,' he greeted me cheerily.

He was looking well, all togged up in a three-piece pinstripe suit. He had an appointment with the bank manager about a loan.

'I never asked you,' I said. 'Who was the best you ever played against?'

The corners of his lips twitched up at the memory.

'Jimmy White. I was twenty-nine, he was twenty-two. I felt him coming at me like a boxer,' he said, his shoulders rolling with the ghost of a boxer's feint. 'Of the current crop Ronnie O'Sullivan but he's thrown it away. Ronnie's problem is cocaine and women. I didn't do cocaine. I was maligned by the press.'

Grievance was setting in again so I said nothing more to fuel it.

The bus came and we got on. Alex insisted on paying for my ticket.

'Strange I should bump into you again this soon.'

I agreed it was. Even though we lived near to each other it was easy to lose people in Belfast.

'I don't have much energy now for all that business, so I must have really fancied you,' he confided. 'I was really randy that night. Are you seeing anyone now?'

'Well, one man keeps texting me but I've already told him I'm not interested.'

'Perhaps he doesn't want consensual sex. Just a sensual text will do him,' said Alex and we both laughed.

A message came through on his mobile and he checked it.

'My jockey. Tips,' he explained. 'Got some sure-fire winners today.'

'I thought the horses weren't working.'

'Oh yeah, I've lost loads but I'm alive, I'm still in the race and the bookies are worried!'

I remembered something about him, how he would let the other player steal the lead, so that on the brink of defeat he could stage a great comeback with the crowd behind him inflamed, impaled on the conviction of his genius.

'Look, I've got to get off soon. Let me give you my number if you ever want to call me.'

He scribbled it down on the back of the ticket and handed it to me.

No one spared him a second glance as he left. Why should they? He had that haggard complexion of the wrecks down the pubs who'd never achieved much but talked as though they had and he could well have been going in his suit to the funeral of one of his short-lived compatriots.

I watched him alight and he turned and came alongside the bus. Something was perceptibly different. He had a cocky attitude to his step and he grinned up at me and rapped on my window with a speed that made me jump. For a second, strutting along in his sharp-cut suit, it could have been the young Alex and with that scribbled phone number he'd slammed in the black and won the frame, keeping the game alive, and, God, he knew he still had it, had me and I twisted round in my seat to capture a final look at him. His suit shivered under the breath of the enormous sky, the strut expanded across the deserted acreage of pavement and I lost him as the bus shrugged on its way.

CATHOLIC BOY

Jarlath lay in Ruth's bed. Those red lips slightly parted like they were anxious to keep tasting the world. That disparity between white unblemished skin and masculine muscle. He came from the other side of the peace line and it didn't faze either of them.

'What's that noise?' he asked, sitting up suddenly.

She listened for a second, half-expecting it might be the screeches from the drunken pickups that her housemate, Colin, habitually brought back with him from the clubs on a Friday night. The Decibel Jezebels as she jokingly termed them behind Colin's back. Then she realised it was nothing but the usual creaking from the derelict house next door where the outer wall had been bulldozed. You could hear the wind run up the stairs, spiral the lampshade, peel back the wallpaper, playing with the house at its delinquent leisure.

'You know I'm thirty-seven,' Ruth told him, knowing he was only nineteen.

'You'd better take control then.'

Ruth had met him earlier that night in Kelly's Cellars after she'd called in with a friend, Sinead, from work. He was sitting in the trad session group playing the Irish pipes and the first thing that struck her was the curls that obscured his face as he looked down in concentration at his fingers. She couldn't help noticing the leather strap tightened around his upper arm; it was that strap across his white skin that made her long for him indefinably, perhaps in its insinuations of strain and quickened pulse-beat. Desire was triggered off in the subtlest of ways. She and Sinead sat down next to the group in the only seats that were free. When he stopped for a break, she spoke to him.

'Are you wearing lipstick?' she asked, staring at his red lips.

'No, it's all natural, I swear to you,' he replied, taking it in his stride, though he fidgeted nervously with the hippyish bead bracelet he was wearing.

'I thought you were gay for a minute.'

'Hit her, Jarlath,' Sinead interrupted with a gasp.

'Some girls have thought that but they soon changed their minds and left very satisfied,' he answered and his bravado suited her. A look had been exchanged, the lightest and least binding of contracts, but nevertheless it was there.

His sister was playing the fiddle. When Jarlath went to get a drink at the bar, Ruth talked to the sister who had long dark hair and soft brown eyes. Somehow getting on well with a member of his family ratified him. But she guessed that even murderers occasionally went out for a pint with their sisters, so that blew that theory out of the water. Still, she couldn't help feeling that if she'd been born a man she would have been attracted to Jarlath's sister, so there was a symmetry in this meeting, a kind of double desire that made her want Jarlath more.

'Hello, wee darlin',' an elderly man with a clapped-in mouth was shouting at Ruth and he triggered his finger into the air and began to sing a Republican anthem.

'Shhh,' said the bar owner, coming out from behind the bar.

The old man stood over her, his eyes fixed on her, his mouth moving in a scarcely discernible whisper, repeating the same lip movements over and over, as in a rosary. The Mighty Quinn was his name, Jarlath said.

'Do you know what he's saying?' asked Jarlath, to which she shook her head. '"Up the Provies", over and over.'

And it began, the bed concerto, the high-pitched fiddling of the loose wooden frame, the base pounding of the mattress and spring percussion and it blotted out the infernal acoustics of the wind next door, as though his breathy gasps and 'yeahs' were competing and driving the wind away like bad spirits. In a rare pause, she marvelled at him in her bed, as if he didn't belong in this crumbling, three-storey Victorian house, his peerless skin dazzling against the stained wall.

'You're beautiful,' she told him.

'Don't.'

His face flinched and she could have kicked herself. Hearing from older men that she was beautiful when she was young had irritated her too.

'So, did you like me the moment you first saw me?' she asked, willing him to say something good.

'Yeah.'

He was vacant, sightless, still lost in the feelings of his own body. The door of the neighbouring house had been wrenched by the wind and was banging like an invitation for unwanted guests to leave.

He had to go, he said, as he had an appointment at a recording studio in the morning and she was glad because there was no conversation between them. He got dressed quickly and shyly like he was in a public place and not her bedroom, so aware was he of her eyes taking everything in. He didn't want her to walk him to the front door and she smiled as she heard him clumsily descend the stairs. As she slowly fell asleep, she couldn't tell if the creaking she heard came from the springs in the mattress unaccustomed to so much strenuous exercise or the lists of her tired, drugged-up head. The solitary dark always brought a fear of hallucinations with it. The fear lay in the danger that one night the little zips of spinning light in the darkness would become her reality, supplanting the normal day-to-day vision, trapping her in their sparkling blindness forever.

Morning came and she stretched luxuriantly, feeling trium-phantly sexual. As she pulled back the curtains from the rheumy eye of the old window, she spied his scarf lying under the table. It smelled of perfume and not him. She put it round her neck, but couldn't manage to knot it as he had done, which somehow bothered her. She remembered a fifty-year-old she'd slept with who'd said that young people to him now were like beautiful ponies; they no longer attracted him. She almost pitied that fifty-year-old, what a madman, giving up on beauty. When she checked herself in the mirror she could have sworn she looked younger. The light reflecting off the sun-browned curtains gave a warmth to her skin and faded the veins and blemishes, as if she had undergone a rejuvenescence overnight. Suddenly she thought she could detect the chemical aroma of condoms and threw open the window. Shivering, she got ready to go out.

It was a freezing December day, 'dark and dirty,' as her father would have said, enlivened only by the jangling of plastic icicles festooning eaves and the sight of inflatable Santas doing shimmies up drainpipes. The Christmas lights lay dark, like empty bottles after a party. The sole brightness in the sky came from the white plumes of steam from the engineering works. She passed the neighbouring house, showing its entrails like a home interior exhibition hit by vandals. Half the houses in the street had been condemned by the Housing Executive and their windows breeze-blocked. The front doors encased in brown metal and stamped with official warnings of impending demolition reminded her of prematurely erected gravestones. Old bunting hung tangled and noosed above the doors. Ironically one of the condemned houses bore a blue plaque, bearing the words, 'Best Kept Street, Belfast City Council 1991,' and she was suddenly reminded of the old Republican's crowing in Kelly's Cellars: 'They said that the grass would never grow on the shipyard and look at it now!'

At the Methodist church, a huge sign said 'Hooked on Jesus.' On the wall opposite was scrawled 'New Land Outlaws', indicating how the people of these streets were torn between religion and gangsterism.

She went into a small cafe, its windows curtained with steam and ordered a fry. The ache in her legs and womb as she sat down reminded her of the sex and made her happy. Medication for urban depression, she told herself. She found herself gazing at the plate on the counter, full of fairy cakes, iced with pallid lemon and anaemic pink. She watched the wee hard women busy themselves around the counter, their voices grown harsh from hooshing their drunken men at home, and the cosy familiarity washed over her. Framed photos of hot cross buns in Easter baskets adorned the mock-ecclesiastical arches in the wall.

In the taxi home, Sinead asked, 'What are yous two up to under there?'

Ruth brought Jarlath's hand out from under the pipes case.

'Nothing, just holding hands,' she lied and Jarlath's other hand crept across her thigh. Ruth looked up at the night, her heart soaring. It was moments like these that made it worthwhile, the nights of touring bar after bar, searching, playing this 'pass the parcel' existence, unwrapping experience after experience and finding emptiness inside. For once the night held something. The taxi driver kept braking as drunken girls tottered across the road like newborn foals, their bare legs fawn with fake tan and tipped with white shoes.

The city was alive.

Pasty-looking men kept entering the cafe, their faces wrecked through self-demolition by alcohol. They were the familiar casualties of hard partying and the single life, needing urgent resuscitation by greasy fry.

'Sure, why drink water when you can drink beer?' one of the diners was pontificating loudly. 'Water rots wood and rusts metal, so why would you ever put it into you?'

Ruth hugged Jarlath's scarf to her chest. She began to think of a line of typical tongue-in-cheek sexual vaunting to entertain the girls in the pub with later: *having young guys in your bed keeps you young— but I'm not throwing the moisturiser out just yet.* It was a bit lame but something better would come to mind later and anyway it would come across okay with the right inflections. There were always two voices in Ruth's head commenting on her actions — one the rather anxious voice of reality and the other rehearsing for later performance.

But at the same time she thought how the whole act of possessing someone for a night, of 'having to have them' was futile, unmanageable, a kind of consumeristic nihilism. No one was possessable through sex any more than the mind of a favourite writer was attainable through the reading of their work. And yet, so many women had brought down presidents and leaders by pinpointing some description, some giveaway act that was unique to the man. To have sex with someone was akin to knowing their genetic blueprint. There was no greater intimacy — and paradoxically no greater distance. The ultimate problem in having sex with a stranger was that you were exploring their body but incapable of knowing anything about their mind, in the warmth and cold at once, within them and yet outside them entirely. Yes, possession wasn't easy... The memory came back of the sudden panic as he was leaving, of where the condom was, and then pulling it out from inside her, peeling it away like a second skin.

She smelt the scarf and the sweetness from it reassured her. She knew that Jarlath lived in the next street to Sinead and she had a ready-made excuse in returning the scarf. Perhaps he'd left it on purpose as many men did; some even said to her on the way out when she'd spotted their gloves or socks, that they would get them *the next time.* She prided herself on the fact that they always wanted to come back. Yet with Jarlath she really wasn't sure that he would want to and, strangely, it felt like a betrayal. For this reason alone, she thought she should see him, *stir* him. She stood up quickly. Oh, it was asking for disappointment but at the same time her own madness excited her.

Some snow had fallen on the dry malty-coloured mountains, making them look like floury wheaten farls. It was three o'clock and the layered clouds snagged by the wind had taken on a lurid infected orange tinge. The orange inflamed suddenly into pink and then, cooled by the impending darkness, turned back to a downy white. Ruth hurried up the Limestone Road past the meshes denoting the peace line that grew taller every summer. Although she was in Nationalist territory, the streets were littered with tribal remains of her side. Heather's Mini-Market lay derelict, Adair and Milliken Engineering was chained up and empty. These monuments came from businesses burnt out only in the past few years.

She couldn't help her anger. She often thought herself fluid, accepting, tolerant but the illusion of being well-balanced came from the fact that she could swing from one extreme to the other — one day she was conservative, one day socialist, one day Christian, one day atheist, one day she was with the Protestants understanding their grievances, the next with the Catholics, understanding theirs... open-mindedness meant that she felt the truth behind all points of view. The trouble was it made her doubly angry instead of tolerant. Up in the stark branches of a tree, a nest rocked like a cradle.

Nerves flew to her stomach as she rang the doorbell. She felt so vulnerable standing there, every window trained on her, and she half-prayed he would answer, half-hoped no one was in. Before she had a chance to turn, a girl opened the door, dark-haired and brown-eyed.

Ruth had been expecting housemates. She was shocked. Was it another older sister?

'I'm afraid he went out,' the girl said and, as Ruth became accustomed to the artificial light in the hall, it revealed the comfortable domesticity of the décor and suddenly unveiled the wrinkles in the girl's face, grey hairs in the cornerstones of her temples. It's Jarlath's mother, she realised aghast.

'He left his scarf,' she gabbled quickly, taking it off and passing it to the woman.

In those seconds she took in the confused quiver of the woman's plucked eyebrows, surveying her face for its remains of beauty. She was struck with the crazy impression of meeting a rival in love rather than his mother.

'I'll give it to him,' said the woman in a kind but bemused way, looking at Ruth as though trying to place her from some long-past memory.

Ruth's face was burning as she fled back onto the street.

People passed by, hunched, shouldering the winter darkness like a coffin. She zipped up her coat feeling an instant chill. In the scarf's soft hook had lain the only chance of seeing him again. She remembered the childish excitement in his voice as he'd told her he was going to study medicine at university that autumn and the cold fear returned. She knew she needed a chemist's to get the pill to take the dread away, to erase that drunken night.

As she hurried, she couldn't help but remember the sound of him in sex; the sighs and the moans, soaking up her sexual pleasure, reflecting her own deep-throated murmurs. Something to hold, something to hold on to. Against the Nationalist side of the peace line, a youth lolled, following her with his eyes, his mouth moving over and over, the words drowned by traffic, the frosty condensation hitting the air like the spray of graffiti.

THE ART OF MENDACITY

And so I went round to see Caroline's flat. Guess I just fancied a change from some flophouse or Grim Reaper's bedsit. Somewhere more like home for a change. I should have remembered from years back that home comforts mean a sacrifice in freedom.

Caroline was pleasant but a bit nervous about the prospect of taking on a DSS person. Stands for dole-scamming scrounger in her book, but fortunately I don't conform to the breed. I don't have a lazy posture or shifty eyes.

'So, what do you do with yourself all day if you don't work?' she'd asked me, kind of suspiciously.

'Oh, devil worship, sacrifice a few chickens, drill holes in walls, play with myself from morning to night,' I'd been tempted to say, but instead I said brightly, 'I write.'

I knew this would please her. A nice, quiet hobby. She'll be no problem, I imagined her saying to her friends. She'll be in her room writing all day.

'What sort of things? Novels?'

'Oh, all sorts,' I replied.

'Sorry if I seem intrusive,' she said, relaxing. 'But I have to make sure what sort of person you are. You hear some terrible tales about letting people into your home. I knew someone who came home once to find her flatmate had stripped the whole place and absconded.'

I took a look at the dinky ornaments on her mantelpiece. 'I don't think you need worry,' I assured her.

Anyway she took me on. I think it was because she knew that she wouldn't have to fight with me for the bathroom in the mornings. She took a horrendously long time to get ready. I'm sure she put scaffolding on her face before laying on the make-up. While all this went on though, I was peacefully akip.

One thing I found out very soon was that she was flat-proud. Flat-obsessed even. She was so afraid of the demon damp taking a foothold in her flat, that you had to cook with the window open even when it was blowing a force nine. Not using a coaster was a crime punishable by the whip of a tea towel. As for a stain on the carpet or settee... Now if I was like her, I would have brown patterned stuff, not a settee like a cream bun which is asking for trouble, but some people seem to thrive on a difficult life.

Funnily enough we got on. I looked forward to her coming home in the evenings. I liked her talking about her day at the office. I'd have a meal prepared, she'd open the wine, she'd phone me if she was going to be late home. 'It's almost like you're my wife,' she'd laugh.

'Cept I wasn't of course. Which brings me on to the real problem of living with Caroline. I had this lifestyle of kicking it around the streets and pubs, so it wasn't surprising that I'd hook up with a few men now and again. Caroline made her view very clear at the start.

'Now, I don't want any strange men coming and going here,' she said, looking protectively at her ornaments again. 'A boyfriend's fine. All I want to do is meet him and if he's a nice, decent boy, you can have him over as much as you want. I'm not a complete killjoy, you know.'

Only a ninety-nine per cent one. She put the pure right back into puritan. She was only three years older than me too.

Boyfriend. I hadn't heard this word since I was about sixteen. I had this amusing image of introducing her to some of the unusual characters that I knew and letting her vet them. Vet sounded very painful. Like she'd be giving them the snip or something.

There was one other drawback to the flat. It was the upstairs neighbours who had two brattish kids and a dog and they packed so much weight they made the ceiling lamp swing with every footstep. The Richterometer, I called that lamp. The man was a DIY fanatic which in his case meant Destroy It Yourself. Had a thing against walls — theirs must have been the only totally open-plan flat in the city. I mean, what if I really had been a writer like I told Caroline and they'd interrupted my great works? So what I did some afternoons for fun was keep bouncing a tennis ball against the ceiling to annoy them back and cranked up the television to ear-splitting level. The woman once came down to complain about the racket and said, 'If my man was here, he'd tell you what was what.'

Well, that really made me tremble. 'Well, tremble my tailfeathers,' I'd said to her and she'd stomped off muttering some American talk-show garbage about all having to live together.

I honestly tried for the first month to comply with Caroline's house rules, but in the end lust got the better of me. Brought back to the flat on an afternoon, there were:

Jonathan, who I met on the train. He made a lot of moans during sex. Made the dog howl upstairs.

Craig. We had fun taking some tasteful eroto-photo-portraits of one another on our mobiles but always caution over pleasure. I surreptitiously deleted his before he left.

Tommy, the joiner, who freaked me out when he put his work boots on Caroline's sofa. Big on action, not talk. 'Now, don't try and get into my head,' he told me, when I asked him a question once. As he'd just entered my body, I didn't see why he shouldn't permit me similar access to his mind.

Isaac, who I met in the metro station. Big and black. One giant chunk of Afrodisiac. He was asleep when Caroline came home early one day and I had to pummel him awake and smuggle him out.

Cameron with his mirror-perfected smile. Too good-looking, as some girls would say. But I always say there is no such thing as too good-looking, only too ugly. There is a general assumption among women that a bloke blessed on the looks front has no personality, is hopelessly vain, and is a born cheater. I pay no attention to this. It is simply a conspiracy by ugly women to stop the rest of us having the good-looking ones.

So the flat suited me very well. But after a little while I discovered I'd been a touch rash in making enemies of the people upstairs.

One night Caroline came in and there were no smiles for me. The woman upstairs had told her that I'd been busy entertaining all manner of men and there'd been comings and goings from breakfast to tea time and these goings-on were disgraceful.

I could see the front door of the flat looming large with a bright exit sign above it, but I wasn't prepared to give up without a fight.

'Surely, you don't believe her,' I'd replied. 'All I've had is some female friends round on an occasional afternoon and so what if a couple of them have brought their boyfriends? How can she tell who comes here unless she stands at the window from dawn till dusk?'

Caroline nodded and I pressed home my advantage. After all, I wasn't a bad flatmate and her tea was in the oven. Soon I had Caroline convinced that the woman was simply jealous of our friendship. We even started having a bit of a laugh about the woman. Her name was Dawn Lumsden. You're joking, I said. Mrs Lumsden. Half-way between glum and a lump. The Lumpenproletariats upstairs.

But a little bit of trust had been lost. Every evening Caroline started to ask me what I'd done during the day. I had to tell her I had writer's block and that no medication seemed to shift it. A couple of days later, she said, 'Isn't it time you looked for a job?'

'What for?' I said. 'Regard the lilies of the field, they toil not, neither do they spin, but they look bloody lovely. That's me.'

She thought that flippant. She even brought home a paper with jobs she'd circled. 'Here's one for you,' she said, pointing to an advert that said, 'Salespeople with bubbly personality required.'

'I do not bubble, I do not even effervesce, except on the inside after five pints of lager,' I told her and she finally took the hint.

But what Caroline didn't understand was that all of us on benefits already do have careers. For instance, I have a sexual career that keeps me very busy; similarly, other people have a drug or a thieving career into which they invest all their energies. We don't just *do nothing*.

I decided to cool it on the man front for a while. But just like a serial killer knows the desires will eventually become too much, I, a serial sleeper, knew I'd eventually bring back someone else. In the meantime I went out of my way to please her. I even changed out of my house-jumper when she had friends round, because she said it was a state. (Looks like it's had more hot meals than I've had! One of these days it'll start crawling on its elbows to the washing machine!) And I didn't balk when she picked out one of her own shirts for me to wear. 'Looks very prissy,' I observed, though, when I had a look at myself. 'Yes, it is pretty, isn't it? It suits you,' she said, surveying me happily. And I have to admit I liked it when she was pleased and I almost liked it when she was displeased too because it meant she cared. It seemed years since I inhabited a world where not washing the brown rings properly out of a cup was a terrible thing. It made a pleasant change to think about the importance of wiping down the microwave instead of wondering what to do next for kicks.

I liked observing her. Truly she fascinated me. She wore clothes with names like bodies and teddies and expensive perfumes and embrocations of which I knew nothing. She was so intensely feminine as to make my own femaleness pall. When she had her friends round, I felt like a straight man in the company of camp queens.

But let me just say this, because it seems to me that I'm not coming across very well out of this story. In my defence, Caroline was the sort of person who forced people to lie. For every liar in the world, there is a what you might call a liee.

'What do you think of this?' she'd ask me of some impractical high fashion outfit she'd just slipped on.

She put terrible pressure on me. I mean, we all know it's wrong to lie but we also think there are occasions when little white lies are permissible, even advisable. You'd think the gospel writers would have stuck a few instructional verses on this subject into the *New Testament*, such as where Jesus has on a new robe and says, 'What do you reckon to my new threads then, John?' White lies are a very grey area.

It was the night I was standing waiting at the deserted taxi rank that I met Sammy. He was standing a little way off from me, gangsteresque in appearance with his dark suit and dark hat. I was so surprised when he spoke because they never looked at you let alone spoke to you. Rat-a-tat came the quick fire of solecistic questions delivered with a New York accent. Where you headed? You a boyfriend? What you do for *it* then?

I gave him my phone number, told him to ring me up the next day. At about tenish it was quiet on the streets, so it was fairly safe for him to walk up the alleyways to my flat. He was an Orthodox Jew, studying at a local college. Only nineteen, he was. I was surprised to find such a slender body hidden under the coat, the suit, the jumper, the shirt, the tassled garment and the vest. Like when you complain at Easter that the eggs are all packaging and you don't get much chocolate. Only I didn't complain because I liked how he was boyish. We used to lie in bed and smoke his white-tipped American Marlboros and he'd tell me how back in New York he already had his future bride picked out for him. Immediately he had my sympathy. Somehow I imagined her wearing thick black tights and having a fuzz of facial hair. When he left the flat, he had that hunted-by-the-FBI, furtive look on his face and he would warn me, 'If ever any Jews phone up and ask about me, always deny that you know me.' 'As if you should worry,' I thought. The idea of the Chief Rabbi on the phone to Caroline didn't bear thinking about. Sammy would only have to say a few Hail Judahs, presumably, while I'd be turfed out onto the street.

Times were especially dangerous as the woman upstairs had tripped over her pesky dog when going down the stairs and had bruised her coccyx. It felt like she was upstairs on her cushioned backside just watching.

Roughly speaking, you can classify men into the runners and the stayers and Sammy was definitely a runner. By that, I mean he would run off afterwards plagued by guilt, deciding to call a halt to us. But a few days later I'd get a phone call and he could be very persuasive, could Sammy. I think the fates must have been against us meeting in the first place. I mean, for discretion purposes, I'd have been better off inviting a man wearing an orange tutu to rollerblade up the road to my flat. There was that one morning I opened the back gate as usual for him to sneak in, when I heard this huge braying noise from upstairs. It was my neighbour going to one of her children, 'Did you open that gate again, Andrea? Well, I don't care. Run down and close it.' I might have known the interfering snooper would spoil everything. So, I went out and shouted up to old Snoop Doggy Dog at the window that it was me who'd opened the gate, then I rushed out and told Sammy who was coming up the alley to quickly run round to the front. It was getting ridiculous, all this subterfuge.

One evening, when I let myself into the flat, I heard the familiar tones of our neighbour coming from the living room and I had an immediate feeling of doom. Since I'd moved in, she'd hardly set foot in the flat, but pre me, she'd visited Caroline quite regularly to gloat about how much cheaper her gas bill was. Also, to boast about her great sex life. She and her man had it twice a week – Wednesday nights and Sunday mornings. Caroline had the bedroom underneath theirs, so she knew this without the woman having to tell her. Caroline said it was like living under a train viaduct.

Anyway, no sooner had I come in, than the woman stopped in

mid-sentence and said to me, 'I was just saying to Caroline, did you have a Jew come here the other day?'

Stay calm, I told myself, feeling Caroline's eyes on me.

'No, no,' I said, raising one side of my top lip as if to ask, What are you on about? 'There was no Jew here.'

'Well, that's funny,' said the neighbour. 'My Pete was just driving off in his car the other morning and he was sure he saw a Jew go into this flat.'

'Must have been next door,' I said, protruding my bottom lip and shaking my head, as if in puzzled concentration. Fortunately, I can call on a wonderful array of facial expressions to help me out of a tight corner. People have told me that I look like a young Vanessa Redgrave which may explain the acting ability. Of course, I've also been told that I look like the gay man out of *Hollyoaks*, but I believe he's sufficiently pretty for me not to take offence. I put on my smile with raised eyebrows. 'I mean, I think I would remember if a Jew came to the flat. But funny enough, I have noticed quite a few Hare Krishnas round here recently.'

'No, it wasn't one of them,' said the woman with a final dissecting stare. Once again, she couldn't prove anything. She must have been foaming.

So, I breathed a sigh of relief, finished with Sammy and laid off the men again.

It was a few weeks later while I was running a bath one night that Caroline banged on the door, shouting. What's she heard now, has someone told her the truth about me? was my automatic reaction. I unlocked the door and in she rushed, screaming about all the steam, and wrenching open the window. For once, I'd forgotten the open-window-rule, but it *was* the middle of January. 'Look at the wallpaper,' she screeched, pulling at a scrolled bit up by the ceiling. 'You've made it go curly! You've ruined my flat since you've been here. There's damp everywhere.' I hardly thought this was my fault. I'd had the windows open many a time before she came home to remove the smell of blow.

'Look at this, look at this,' she beckoned, taking me into the kitchen and showing me the stains I'd made on the stainless steel draining board. I couldn't see anything. Then she took me into the living room where, fair enough, hands up on this one, there was a baldy patch on the carpet where I'd dropped the iron. We'd had terrible trouble getting the molten carpet off the iron too. Caroline hadn't forgiven me for the stains like green mould on her best white shirt. 'As for the state of your room,' she raged. 'You've cost me thousands on this flat since you've moved in.'

I couldn't get out of this one, blame it on next door or the people upstairs. She didn't speak to me for the next two days. That's when I decided to move out. You see, it wasn't because of a bloke at all. It wasn't like how I thought it would be.

It was like I could leave with moral integrity intact.

Well, that was until The Very Last Moment.

I was all packed up and I was saying my fond farewells to Caroline in the living room. I was even thinking that she and I weren't so different because, in our own ways, both of us liked to put a nice gloss on things. She said she was sad to see me go and I was just giving it the nice bit about keeping in touch, when I noticed her eyes glaze over and look past me to the backyard. So I turned round to see what was so fascinating out the window. Outside was the bizarre sight of the upstairs kids cracking a whip at the dog. The horror unfurled in my stomach as I immediately recognised it. It had been a present to me, but I'd thrown it out since Sammy had been messing around with it and pulled off the tip.

'Well, it's not bloody mine!' I could hear the woman shouting above. 'It'll be hers downstairs, no doubt. Put it down, Andrea!'

Double horrors! The little kid was holding an envelope of photographs I'd also just thrown out. They bore the indisputable record of the party times I'd had at Caroline's and in particular on Caroline's cream sofa.

'That's me off now,' I said.

PAPER PIRANHAS

Last week I met a guy on the bus who said to me that life was a series of sit-ups. Or was it push-ups? It makes no difference. Or was it star jumps? Fucked if I know anyway. But his point was that the more you get pushed back down, the harder it is to get back up again.

Well, it's Friday afternoon, my first day on this new workfare scheme and I arrive at the offices of the manufacturing company I'm assigned to for the sum total of one week. I don't really know who I'm meant to speak to, but no one seems to bat an eyelid as I walk through the door and start wandering through the open-plan office. I have this impression that I could head straight for the accounts office and exercise a swift hold-up without being challenged. It's only when I start spinning on a big *Mastermind* chair at an empty desk that a woman finally comes over and asks if she can help me.

'I'm here to solve your filing problems,' I say and, unimpressed by my trouble-shooting style, she nods towards the filing cabinet which is being propped up by this morose looking lad dressed in what looks like his old school trousers and shirt but with a bad-taste tie. His hair has a superfluity of natural oils. He brightens perceptibly to see me.

'This place is yawn city,' he warns, dumping this pile of carbon-copied invoices in my arms. We embark on a rapid trot around the offices and he shows me that some invoices go in the cabinets, some on shelves, some in big bookbinders and some in these battered boxes under the stairs. I realise it is not so much a filing system as a filing lottery.

'And the rest go in there, right?' I suggest, pointing to the bin.

'It's quite simple really,' he says, looking at me pityingly. He checks his watch and claps his hands together like celebratory cymbals. 'Right, I'm off home,' he announces. He is very chuffed with the fact that next week he is back working at the Cancer Shop. He says it's a total doss because you sit in the back room drinking tea and rummage through the odd black bag of donations. It's where he pinched his tie from, he says.

So now he's gone, I'm alone with these invoices in my hand, knowing perfectly well I would have needed about five practice runs to memorise where everything goes. For my first afternoon I'd been thinking of nothing more demanding than some gentle-paced salivating on envelopes. I console myself that the boy probably gave me the completely wrong information because in the long line of one dolie explaining the system to the next dolie, the message must end up like Chinese whispers. I look at each member of staff, wondering if I should ask one of them, but they are immersed in their work, so the important thing, I decide, is to look equally busy. Let's face it, it's hard to give a toss when you know you're only there because the company's too stingy to pay someone a weekly wage.

Something about this situation reminds me of the time I took the civil service isometric tests. Logic isn't one of my strong points. I remember this one test that consisted of rows of shapes, like say a squashy-shaped square, then a lopsided triangle, then a pyramidy thing and you had to work out what shape would logically come next. It was a humbling, not to say annihilating, experience. Faced by this cubist nightmare, I drew a couple of jagged blobs, then quietly withdrew from the hall.

For the next couple of hours I file the invoices as best as I can. Whatever's left over I scrunch into the boxes under the stairs. See, who says I have no problem-solving initiative?

I leave the offices early and head back to the flat because I've an appointment at four to do with my new claim for housing benefit. I just moved to this new flat that's owned by a guy I know. He's not really a friend, he has a habit of chuckling over television programmes too much, but I think it will work out for a while.

About a minute after I arrive home, the housing benefit woman turns up. I make her a cup of coffee while she shuffles through papers on her clipboard.

'You move around quite a lot,' she comments suddenly.

'Sorry. I'll sit down with you once the coffee's made,' I say, and a moment later I realise she was referring to my roving lifestyle, but I feel too stupid to admit to this misunderstanding.

'You've been unemployed a year now?' she checks.

I'm amazed. It doesn't seem that long. 'Time flies,' I tell her, 'when you're miserably unfulfilled.' I add the last bit in case she thinks I'm implying that I'm having fun, though the truth is life has been good aboard the DSS Bounty.

She clears her throat and starts filling in more on the form while asking me how many rooms I share in the flat. She has an incredibly long nose like that of an anteater. I wonder if she really quite enjoys nosing around other people's flats. I have an aunt who goes and peers through the windows when she sees that a house is up for sale. Once, she tripped over someone's rockery and twisted her knee in her indomitable quest to find out the quality of a house's inner furnishings.

'Have I not dealt with your claim once before?' she asks, probably thinking of me as a habitual claimant.

'No. Never. Perhaps it was another red-haired person you spoke to.'

She gives me a funny look, but it is true that most regular complexioned people can't distinguish one red-haired and pale-skinned person from another, just as they think all black people look alike. It is a most annoying form of inverted racism.

Scribble, scribble, she keeps going on the clipboard. What a paper-pusher she is. I can't help looking at her fascinatedly every time she takes a sip of her coffee because I'm sure at any second her long nose is going to dip into it.

I start hoping she hasn't read anything about me that would be deleterious to the decision. At one time I used to amuse myself by writing down in my Jobsearch Record names of fictitious companies. It took them about five months to catch on that R. Sole & Sons didn't exist.

'Can you show me your room now, please?' she asks, standing up.

'Certainly.' I take her onto the landing and I start climbing up the stepladder.

'It's up in the attic?' she exclaims, none too thrilled. She is wearing high-heeled shoes. She sort of crawls up the ladder behind me with the close grip and bugged-out eyes of a marmoset scaling a tree. She stops when her head and shoulders are above the floor level, turning her head like a periscope. 'Is this it?' she says.

She is momentarily speechless. There are no windows and the room is entirely bare except for a few pictures, the bed and a small chest of drawers—not forgetting Kieron's vats of homemade beer in the corner. I've agreed to share my room with them in return for sharing them at a later date.

'A room with a brew,' I joke but she's already off back down the ladder.

'Can you show me your landlord's room?' she asks me as I jump nimbly down.

I've never been in Kieron's room. It seems like invading his privacy. There are a couple of posters up of female wrestlers. It makes me think of him suddenly in a different light. You can always tell what animal lives in what burrow or lair by the way they dig it.

'Can I see your rent book?' she next asks and I duly show it to her. With loving care I have forged Kieron's signatures on it. The reason for this is that Kieron is asking thirty-five pounds a week from me and I am asking fifty from the housing benefit people. He doesn't need to know about this.

Next, she wants to see the kitchen where I have already carefully divided our food onto separate shelves in preparation for the woman's inspection. I have even put name tags on our separate cupboards. I have used my noddle and left nothing to chance.

'Do you ever have meals together?' the woman inquires.

How can she ask that having just seen that his cupboard is stacked with identical cans of one portion curry. He has meat curry one night, chicken curry the next and vegetable the next which in his books is a varied diet. Also in his cupboard is a month's supply of Batchelor's Cup-a-Soups. I emphasise the word 'bachelor's' to the woman.

'He did once make me a mushroom cup-a-soup,' I recall, 'but I wouldn't drink it. Have you ever noticed when you put the water in how the powder starts fizzing like some sulphuric geyser? Put me right off.'

'So his name's Kieron, isn't it?' says the woman, slanting her eyes. 'That's Irish. And you're from Northern Ireland, aren't you?'

I'm pretty shocked at this tenuous reason as to why we must be going out together.

'Listen, for a start I'm an Ulster Prod, so I've never been out with so much as a Feargal or a Kieron in my life. Besides, he's from Birmingham if you must know. And no, there's just no way I'd go out with him.'

I think of how I can best communicate to her the unlikelihood of Kieron and me being together. 'Do you watch *Countdown*? You know how they always have that really spoddy dictionary corner. Well then, Kieron would make the ideal 'Guardian of the Dictionary.''

I point to the framed photo of Kieron at his graduation ceremony just to emphasise my point. I feel it is a little unfair on the guy but she has forced me to do it. I wish now I'd put a couple of teddy bears with bows in their hair on my bed to feminise the attic. I realise that she thinks I'm with Kieron because she can't quite believe that anyone could stand living there. Even I acknowledge that it does bear a resemblance to a room in a secure unit for the seriously violent.

'Well, you understand we have to definitely establish that you have no relationship with your landlord,' she justifies herself. 'After all, you say you knew him before you moved in.'

'Only in the loosest sense. I mean, only in the vaguest sense of the word. He was just an acquaintance. In fact, I'll let you read my diary and that'll prove beyond all doubt that I'm not going out with him.'

I'm flustered now and I pick up my diary which is sitting on the table. I leaf through it, looking for a page where it might say I had sex with someone since moving in with Kieron.

'That won't be necessary,' says the woman firmly, heading out towards the stairs.

I hardly hear her. Leafing back, I can't believe it's really that long since I had sex with someone.

I run down the stairs and open the front door for the woman. As she leaves, she looks down at her leg. 'I've got a ladder in my tights now,' she says, her voice sharded with exasperation.

Well, I didn't force her to climb up to the attic, but she gives me a look like she blames me. I wave at her as she drives off.

The week passes quickly. The invoices go into files, perhaps not the right files, but they are filed nonetheless. I spend a lot of my time under the stairs where the boxes are. It's a solitary spot that rather reminds me of my attic room. I have heard rumours from people that the company may soon be going into liquidation, a fact that eases my conscience, as I can't really be doing much damage. At worst I'm just pressing on the accelerator pedal.

On the following Friday I get the letter which says I am not eligible for housing benefit. It's devastating to be told that Kieron and I are believed to be living together but I am too worried to be insulted by the idea. I owe him four weeks rent, so as of today I am homeless.

I get to the office. The morning hangs round like an unwanted guest but I can survive it knowing it's my last day. By two o'clock I am watching the door waiting for my replacement to arrive so I can sneak off home and sort out some sort of temporary accommodation. At three o'clock one of the staff comes over to me. 'Hello, Laura,' he says to me in a bluff, cheery manner and I look down at myself in amazement like I'm the invisible man whose potion has suddenly worn off. For once I exist in this office.

'You have been told, haven't you, that you'll be on here for another week? Your replacement apparently just procured himself a job.'

I can feel my face drop. It's like a custard pie sliding down a wall.

'By the way, Laura, I was just looking for one of this week's invoices and I wasn't able to find it. It's to Green's PLC. Could you bring it to me? It's essential to urgent, I would say.'

It's misplaced to lost, *I* would say.

'I'll sort that out for you straightaway,' I assure him, feeling a little tickle of sweat on my forehead.

I go down to the boxes under the stairs, get down on my hands and knees and practically start ripping through the piles of invoices. I have no idea where anything is. Every neuron in my body's jumping with fear. I'm about to be found out. Then I stop. I stop because it is all over anyway. Like they say, 'when the going gets tough, get going.' Just go, don't damage your self-respect by sticking around.

I slowly walk towards the emergency exit door. I press up on the metal bar and it opens. I feel the cool breeze as I step out onto the road and I remember it was press-ups. Life is a series of press-ups was what the guy on the bus told me. Only he told it wrong because the more you sink down and the more you push back up, the easier it becomes, not the harder. You become stronger. And you know that in the end nothing can stop you rising.

THE IDEAL MAN

This is the year, Jess thought. This year I will get married.

No more fibbers, cheaters, losers, boasters, bleaters, control-freaks or working-class heroes. This year she was going to be ruthless with men and find a good, kind one to settle down with. She was thirty-four, her biological clock was racing, her eggs zinging around in there like ball bearings in a pinball machine. Within a year I plan to be married and pregnant, she said. She even told her friend to be ready at the end of the year to sing 'Ave Maria' at her wedding. And provisionally booked another friend to sing 'Wild Thing'.

Jess threw away all her old business cards with men's numbers (well, she kept one just in case she really did need a plumber one day). She thought of going on an exercise regime but there was really no point in putting herself out of everyone's league and the truth was she stood more of a chance meeting a man down a kebab shop at two thirty a.m. than in a health spa at dawn. Instead, she enrolled in lots and lots of evening classes to meet new people. Finally, at the end of April she found him, or rather stumbled upon him, since they were both lost in the huge, Orwellian education complex.

His name was Stephen and he was a graphic designer and twenty-seven which was perhaps a bit young, but that was okay because he was balding and looked older. Choosing the age of your future partner was a lifestyle choice, rather like choosing to live in the country or in a city. She wasn't fussy about wealth. She didn't insist on a man with his own house and car, just a man with a double bed. The main point was that he was nice and all his friends were going steady with girls, so on the peer pressure front, things were looking good.

He seemed a perfect match except that to him the words 'perfect match' denoted football — it was better than having no interests at all or have them try to hijack your own interests, wasn't it? But then there were those worrying revelations of mental instability in his family, he still went home at the weekend and got his mother to do his washing, and the word 'bitch' featured too much in his vocabulary. Although he knew in Thursday night's pub quiz the name of Queen Elizabeth I's mother, he hadn't a clue about Jess's mother and showed absolutely no inclination to be interested in her family and, besides, balding wasn't the sort of thing you should knowingly pass on genetically to any child.

She didn't sleep with him because she wanted to keep his devotion on the boil. She knew she could change him for the better but it troubled her, especially after her French flatmate mentioned that she was very hard on him. Then one stormy morning she was travelling to work with a hangover and she looked out of her car window and saw a man walking by in the street and the little flap of his jacket lifted up to reveal a perfect ass. She told herself I want a husband, not a perfect ass. And she looked again because thinking about sex always took away the pain of a hangover and saw how the fabric of his suit shuddered and shook with shimmering liquidity up and down his whole body. The party animal in her started to growl though she told it to shut up.

She thought of men slender and carved, looked at the Frenchman she shared a flat with, his skin as honey as halva, a man who could cook and nurture, resinous as sandalwood. Stephen only rented a flat and planned to spend his next paycheck on laser surgery for his eyes, but she wanted a baby soon. Yet, who was perfect? Yes, the Frenchman had curly dark hair she longed to take up in her teeth but he sat talking with his girlfriend for one hour on the phone every night. He looked ideal but he was too clingy, not to mention a little on the short side (which of course would mean you couldn't wear heels on your wedding day) and, anyway, his brother was far too loud and might be a potential embarrassment at family functions.

She was sitting with Stephen watching Jamie Oliver on TV who said, 'Stick it in, pop it in, dip it in, give it a good old shake...' and that was the night it crashed and burned, yearned and spurned and she threw love out in a body bag almost with relief. Stephen cried at first but said he understood and later he left almost cheerfully. 'Thank you for brightening up my summer,' he said, making her feel like a disposable light bulb.

And for the next months she went slumming it, largeing it up joyously on brambling, rootless nights, giving herself up to men with bodies like driftwood. Maybe she was infertile anyway and the whole family thing was a dream. Maybe she'd be better off going to Africa and saving the gorilla. One man asked why she didn't want a relationship and why she'd never been married.

'Because I'm scared of seeing them as ideal or them seeing me as ideal,' she said, stretching out on the faded flowers of the sheet, and that was as close to the truth as it got.

By Christmas she was pale and tired, all partied out and shot to bits. She knew what she wanted now and was determined to get it.

This is the year, Jess thought. This is the year I will get married.

GIANNINO

It was cold outside with a wind that whistled through the ears and nipped at the head. As Vivian unlocked his front door he noticed the man from five doors up staring at him. Vivian hid his unease by pretending that he had trouble with the lock rather than be seen to retreat. Out of the corner of his eye he watched the man disappear inside, the leather jacket curved on his muscular back, black and shiny like a maledictory stone. Mr G. Kearney. Vivian knew his name from the envelope. Kearney was operating a benefits scam whereby he claimed he was living at Vivian's house. Every two weeks he rapped on Vivian's door to collect his giro. Vivian would have loved to tell him where to go but it was wise to be careful who you tackled in West Belfast. Occasionally he recognised in other people the same excuse for physical cowardice.

As he went into the front hall he could hear a yawn unfurling as voluminously as a shout. It always made him smile, this complete incongruity between the loudness and the size of the man. Gianni, his Milanese housemate, was big on yawning, given that he worked nights prepping pizzas.

Gianni didn't turn from pluming the front of his gelled hair in the mirror over the mantelpiece. He had the furrowed, hunted look he always had when seeing to his appearance.

The room smelt of strong, sugared coffee. Gianni waved the menu from the Indian kebab shop in front of Vivian.

'Pizza American, Pizza Tikka Supreme...' rattled off Gianni, almost frothing at the mouth. 'Oh, my God. I say to them you joking or what?' He pushed out his chest and planted an unswerving finger in its centre. 'I professional.'

The revised menu was thrust into Vivian's hands.

Vivian wondered at once if 'Here start new Italian chef Giannino' was a little over-authorial for the top of a pizza menu, but he said nothing.

'Giannino mean little Gianni. How you call in English?'

'A diminutive.'

Gianni shaped his lips to reproduce the word, then thought better of it. 'Zactly,' he said, nodding. 'Ham, salami with a hint of fresh basil,' he read out dreamily, holding out his closed fingertips as if presenting a precious gem for inspection and breathing in the imagined scent of fresh herbs. 'A *hint* of fresh basil. It's the class.'

'Good stuff. I'll get it typed out for you.'

'Thank you.' Gianni buttoned up his coat and growled to himself as he picked up the original menu. 'Fucking dickheads. Professional. So, I'll see you later.'

'See you later, Gianni.'

Gianni turned at the door. 'I am like warrior,' he said, blasting the room with his invisible machine gun and leaving with a grin.

Vivian took the menu up to his room. Sitting on the stairs were Gianni's immaculate tan shoes. Vivian suspected Gianni wore them two sizes too big.

Vivian switched on his computer. It was only when he began to type the actual words that he began chuckling. The menu read like a family tribute and, what was more, each pizza seemed to bear the characteristics of the person. Pizza Giuliana, which was his sister's name, consisted of garlic base, chilli and chicken and Vivian couldn't help conjuring up a slender, pale body, hot and passionate. Michelone, Gianni's friend, was represented by ham, bacon, peppers, chicken and mushrooms. The fact that he had the most ingredients to his name surely testified to his many qualities. As for Pizza Giannino, it was heavy on the meat—ham, salami and pepperoni.

Vivian hurried to the end of the menu. He was anxious to reopen the article he'd been writing. He glanced down at the open page of a library book and reread the sentence he'd underlined in pencil: 'Like Nature itself, Celtic art abhorred a straight line.' He thought about it, his eyes barely focusing on the rows and rows of rectangular bricks in the buildings opposite.

At school he had heard the nuns whisper 'fucking this, fucking that,' round the corners of the corridors and heard the priest refer to 'the Sunday gig'. It made him shiver to remember kneeling among the other children, faces upturned like young birds squawking open-mouthed for the wafer while the old priest, gaunt, stooped, etched, almost Gothic in design, hovered like a black raven. When Vivian had developed epilepsy in his teens, the priest had told his parents it was the devil battling for his soul. Each time he emerged from a fit, his father would be kneeling on his chest and his mother standing over them, hands clasped, reciting the decades of the rosary fervent, monotone and fast like a commentator on a horse race.

Straight lines, straight lines and no colours. That was religious teaching. His parents had been more Irish Catholic than most, naming him Vivian after de Valera's brother. He'd wished they'd called him Eamon after the man himself because he'd taken a gutful of teasing for having a girl's name. The one thing he had really respected about his parents was their tolerance. They had tried hard to protect the Protestants who also lived in the Divis Flats, but one or two of those Protestants were now just names in the lists of The Disappeared.

He wrote quickly, decisively, then titled his piece, 'Voice of the

Gael.' The page pushed out from the printer like a white sheet of ice, curving over the stapler, shaping mountainously. A tremendous excitement came over him. What he was writing was important not in terms of intrinsic merit but of people's reaction. It was not by demonstrating your own argument but by provoking an illogical rage in others that you knew you were writing the truth.

He'd had terrible nightmares in his childhood as a precursor to his fits. At one stage he'd been too afraid to sleep and his mother had again consulted the priest whose professional opinion was that Vivian had dabbled in the occult and should pray in church every day until his soul was absolved. When Vivian had a dream now, it was still tinged with guilt and shame.

However, on this particular night the dream had to do less with putative dark forces than with the real. Through a muddled reel of visions, he saw himself shot twice in the chest by masked men and the panic woke him up in a sweat in the too-warm room.

He moved his head towards the bright waterfall of curtains, cold from the window's draft. The nightmare was to do with his writing. On publication of his previous article three months ago in *The Irish News*, a calling card had been put through his letterbox. It was a small condolence card of the type usually sent with a wreath and this one carried the message scrawled in felt tip, 'Watch out. Dead Gael walking.' The sick humour was proof in itself that the threat came from the paramilitaries, not just a few rogue hoods. It had shocked him. Admittedly he had been laying into the IRA as well as the church and a whiff of apostasy was polemic to the fundamentalists even in this era of peace. The words of his latest article returned to him:

'Our Celtic ancestors buried their sacrificial victims in bogs to appease the gods of nature, whereas the Provies dumped their victims unceremoniously, godlessly, in an effort to hide their acts. The legacy of The Disappeared proves the IRA were the enemies of Ireland.'

His mouth had turned dry. Calm down, he told himself. He could always phone the paper and tell them to pull the article. It wasn't too late.

He tried to relax but the adrenalin was still there. And the heat. Gianni must have switched on the heating. Sometimes Vivian could have sworn that all that garlic Gianni cooked was passing up through the pipes into his room.

No, there was no chance of any more sleep.

He went down the stairs quietly. Last week he had uncovered the secret of Gianni's Latino tan when he'd stumbled upon him in the living room snoring bare-chested under a sunlamp. Just in time he'd roused Gianni who'd had to dab calamine lotion on his pink face for the next few days.

'Hey, Johnny, there's someone here,' said a female voice in a broad Belfast accent as he opened the living room door.

It was almost proprietorial in manner, as if Vivian was the interloper in a love snug.

'S'okay, s'okay,' Gianni said softly, tapping her on the knee.

'Where's the fags?' asked the girl abruptly.

Vivian sneaked a quick look at the girl baring her midriff like a tan belt. Her mascara had run from the rain. He didn't know where Gianni picked these girls up.

Gianni tutted, irritated by his housemate being in night after night.

Vivian went through to the bathroom and switched on the light. It was merciless, cruel, illuminating his head, bald and misshapen as a ball of dough rolled by hand. His nose was slightly off-kilter like a flag planted by a wonky surveyor. He touched the indentations on his forehead. The epileptic fits over the years had caused him to fracture his skull twice and he could still feel the staple in his brow. He felt a huge wave of self-pity. That was why he couldn't work and why no woman could ever live with him. He was already so lucky to have survived he wasn't going to hold back in his writing, whatever the consequences. He resolved to go ahead with the article.

When he went back through, they had disappeared. As he passed Gianni's room he could see the red light under the badly fitting door and overheard a low snuffle of desire.

It was the afternoon the article was due to be published and Vivian was getting ready to go out.

Gianni had woken up at two o'clock. Vivian could tell the exact time by the cockerel-like cry from Gianni's room that signalled the first stretch of the shoulders. He was now up, having just prepared his cup of coffee and was still crinkle-eyed from the pain of the light. His voice was deep, smoky, monosyllabic like Edith Piaf on a downer. He was mooching around with the zip of his jeans down when he suddenly saw the mouse, or the 'mouth' as he called it, run into the kitchen.

Vivian debated whether or not to pull the bin out but thought better of it. In this house you wouldn't move anything for fear of what could be living under it. Anyone who entered believed the heady smell came from a burnt joss stick but really it was the smell of an aromatic strain of damp. In a way it was surprising that the mouse hadn't chosen somewhere better to live. Vivian set one trap beside the cooker and the other beside the washing machine.

'Tell you what, you need the glue. It better. It catch the mouth's feet and it can't go away,' Gianni's voice trailed in from the living room.

Vivian didn't answer, momentarily amusing himself with the vision of the mouse nesting in one of Gianni's Italian shoes.

Gianni was sitting back with his shirt off, spraying himself with Armani and Valentino aftershave and taking long satisfied sniffs at his own arms. The espresso cup at his feet had been drained.

'What you fink that girl last night? Beautiful, no?'

'Beautiful.'

'You no is stallion like me, huh? Believe me what, very nice party here last night. Very nice organise.'

'That's the fifth girl this week.'

'Oh, sex, I lova it, you understand my way? Anyway, it no so many,' shrugged Gianni modestly. 'I Casanova shining.'

'Shy Casanova,' corrected Vivian.

'Casanova shining.'

He laid his head back and wagged his finger at the heavens as if admonishing a naughty boy for making him do things he regretted.

He then flashed Vivian the familiar smile, his upper lip covering his top teeth but revealing the side teeth, glimmering in the dingy living room as Vivian imagined they would in a nightclub.

'Hey, you know dickhead who come round here for giro? Tell you what, that wanker not coming here any more. I break the face. Bam-bam!' he grinned, shelling his fist in his other hand.

Vivian tried to tell him Kearney might have paramilitary connections but Gianni just laughed, pulling his hand up his arm in an imitation of someone loading a gun.

'Madonna mia, you joking or what?'

He switched on the stereo and began whistling like a demented budgerigar to dance music. Then he sprayed himself with the Armani some more as if fuelling himself with all the senses for the long steaming night in the pizza-kebab house.

As Vivian headed out, the rain was just stopping. The final cloud-shadows had rolled over the edge of the mountains and were moving across the green terrain like a dark landslide followed by the sun. In this country you could slip between seasons in a second. It occurred to him that the Celts had believed in the same fluidity and he was pleased enough by the link to allow himself a moment's self-congratulation. As the Celts saw it, there existed opposite worlds side by side which could be visited through natural portals like oak trees and raths.

When he got to the shop he picked up the *Andersonstown News* and flicked to the Arts Section. His article was there. It was there! Pride and fear shot through him.

'It's cleared up rightly now,' said the elderly shopkeeper, peering curiously at him across the counter.

Vivian quickly folded up the newspaper, put the coins into a hand stained ochre from tobacco and hurried into the sunlight. Outside, the brown mossy roofs and sun-warmed bricks merged with the muddy-green mountains cauled with burnt orange ferns. The old plump bricks were like loaves with their edges picked at by small fingers.

Suddenly he felt incredibly happy. 'La donna italiana, la donna italiana,' he repeated to himself revelling in the melody of the accent. In the back of his brain the plethora of old words such as sin, iniquity, abhorrent, shame, most grievous, words that crept upon him like stealthy puritans whenever he had enjoyed himself in the past, stirred uncomfortably, then fled.

He suddenly let out a bray, the same kind of compulsively edgy whinny that Gianni would let out while dancing to his Italian music. He didn't care about the danger any more. He noticed the leaves skelter down the road and looking at them made him hungry. They were the colour of batter, of tempura, thin-sliced delicacies skewered on a stem and deep-fried in the oily puddles. He longed to slither them up through his teeth as Gianni did with spaghetti. He was ravenous. He realised he'd been so wrapped up in the writing he hadn't paid attention to the groans and whines of his body.

Gianni pointed to a small brown mouse that had its vital organs crushed by the trap.

'I fink she pregnant was,' said Gianni, extricating the carcass from the trap and throwing it out into the back alley.

'You look like the mafia,' said Vivian, taking in Gianni's black waistcoat and jacket.

'You fink?' Gianni's eyes swayed across his face, checking for sarcasm. 'This Milan style. Suit with jeans. How much you fink this costed?'

He showed Vivian the labels behind his neck, then, to show the name on his soles, he kicked up his shoes like a well-shod pony to a stable-hand.

'You have a date?'

'Oh, my God. You joking or what. Of course!' Gianni suddenly pulled out of his normal expansiveness. 'But believe me what, Vivian, I tired. What I really want is the wife, children, I'm swear to God. Every day I pray to God and Mary and Padre Pio to send me nice woman. Normal woman. That is my desire. You know, sometime I stop, go into the church, light candle and...' He kissed his hand lovingly and raised it to the sky. 'Why you no send me woman, God? What I done bad? I no kill nobody. You understand the thinking? I'm swear to God. 'Oh, Italia, Oh, Italia,' go the women...'

He pretended to dance, chin tilted up, eyes closed like one of the shallow, enamoured girls he dated. He was no longer looking at Vivian but Vivian was still held in the thrall of his world. Vivian made his own silent prayer to have one night with one of Gianni's rough women.

'Gesù Cristo, I show you.' Suddenly Gianni dropped his trousers.

Vivian didn't know where to look. He hadn't a clue what was happening.

'See?'

Vivian burst into laughter.

On Gianni's inner thigh, obscured by black hairs, was a tattoo of the head of Jesus Christ. It was a sentimental, doe-eyed version of the Man himself, of the type favoured by older ladies of the church, and He was rolling His eyes heavenwards in the general direction of Gianni's crotch.

Gianni winked at Vivian and pointed vaguely to the area in question.

'And I have small tattoo here. It reserve for special baby...'

Later that evening when Vivian was alone in the house he returned to his book.

'Celtic worship venerated the animate,' he read. He finished the bit about shape-shifting into animal form but with a grimace he skipped the chapter about human sacrifice and started on the section about signposts to the other world and the mist summoned by the druids.

Suddenly a loud shattering came from the living room below, jolting the book out of his hands. He rushed downstairs. A brick was lying on the rug, glass everywhere.

This time there was no message.

He felt the darkness stand over him. The fear gripped him that next time they would come and get him. By questioning the sacrifice of the people of West Belfast, he was sacrificing himself. Ironically by harking back to a pre-Christian era, he was turning himself into an anti-Christ. It was almost as if he was embracing the old IRA ideal of martyrdom itself. That was the last thing he wanted. He wanted to live as long as his stapled, friable skull would continue to hold out. He wanted to enjoy his life.

He swept the glass up, thinking it a pitifully fragile protection from the underworld.

At three o'clock he awoke, his eyes springing open in the darkness laced with streetlight. His breath was caught in the burrow of his throat. A door banged below. He leant up on his elbows, ears pricked, dreading the thump of feet on the stairs but nothing came except a muted murmur of voices, one Gianni's, one female. The light, poppy rhythm of Rihanna suddenly danced out from the downstairs stereo.

Back from his walk, Vivian opened the front door and a gust of wind spiralled crisp leaves over the threshold past his feet. A delicious smell of salty meat and garlic filled the hall making his nostrils flare.

In the kitchen Gianni had his head down grating parmesan. He swung round to reveal a viciously swollen black eye.

'What happened, Gianni?'

'Some wanker from here. I was talking to beautiful girl in bar, I went to toilet. Ba-boom, he smack. He must follow me. I fink it was jealous.'

Vivian pictured Gianni open-stanced, garrulous at the bar, his pleasure radiating as arrogance.

Gianni walked over to the mirror above the mantelpiece.

'They crazy bastards round here. Don't know how to enjoy,' he mumbled, turning his face in the mirror, pushing his nose to one side and pointing at the corner of his nostril. 'Look, look, Vivian. Was not like that before.'

'What?'

'It's horrible, no?'

As far as Vivian could see, the nose was exactly the same as before.

Gianni pushed up the front of his nose into a snout and came closer.

'Vines, vines,' he wailed.

Vivian spotted a thread of red no bigger than a spider leg.

'Oh, veins.'

'Yes, vines. Tell me what, is normal? I don't think so!'

Conscious that his own face was a mass of tiny pinpricks of red, Vivian wondered at Gianni's lack of tact.

'Anyway, I will get coh, coh...'

Vivian smiled as the word sprang into his head. As usual Gianni was staring at his lips with an admiring intensity.

'Compensation.'

'Ah, yes. Comp-what-you-say.'

Part of Gianni's charm, realised Vivian, lay in the fact that he didn't make an effort with his English. Gianni would always have that childlike ignorance that would make people want to mother him.

'Come here, come here,' Gianni said, ushering him into the kitchen. He opened the oven and pulled out a magnificent pizza bathed in aromatic steam, misting the room. Vivian experienced a strange tug, a kind of liminal pull to another person's world that made him dizzy for a second, then passed.

'This pizza for you, my friend. You are brave man. Your articles. Ah, we will fight them, yes? You and me, Rocky Balboa,' joked Gianni, dodging like a boxer but rolling his eyes. He took the remaining lump of parmesan in his fist and crumbled it into pale, dry fragments the complexion of his own palm and drizzled them over the pizza, breathing in deep and waggling his chin as though lifted on a thermal to heaven.

Vivian realised then that the real way into a new world was not through religion or beliefs or ideas but through people.

Gianni put his arm around Vivian's shoulders.

'This pizza in honour for you. Salami, pepperoni, olives. Know what I call it? La Mia Vittoria. That mean...' His eyes crinkled. 'My Victory.'

ONE CITY, TWO TOURS

A French fry. Another. Like nuzzling into a bag of straw. American, thought Glen dispassionately, looking at the child's supersized face.

Time to stop staring as the tour bus was already clattering away. He felt the jolt-jolt-jolt in his thin frame. Tap, tap, tap on his microphone.

Good afternoon, ladies and gentlemen, boys and girls, how's about ye?

A few responses but, Jesus, you'd have to run around pure naked to get a gander off this lot. A huddle of Hispanic girls sitting in the open back of the bus. The Americans foundered, plucking at their fries. Aye, he'd hard to work on this tour.

The bus started speeding up towards the Lagan and the Blue Fish. The skies were white as soft soda bread. A mention of the Marriott as they'd sponsored the tour. An even quicker mention of the Titanic and how it was an Englishman who sank it. Sparking out bits of Belfast black humour about how the Europa was the most bombed hotel in Europe.

Then turning mountainward. Up the Falls and pointing out the bullet holes as they crawled past St Mary's. The tourists oohed and aahed and loved the scare of it, but the bus never stayed long on the Falls. At the first opportunity, it turned its back on history and made straight for the peace wall, decorated in flowers and birds and butterflies, looking like a playschool wall instead of a major battlement. Then onto the safety of the Shankill with its oul familiar stories and today the riotous autumn leaves raced along with the bus as it crossed the border and a sudden shaft of light spilled out of the clouds and the heath on the mountain top shone gold, the furze lit up lower down, and the Spanish girls cracked more smiles and even the Americans, fries finished, belched a few laughs and the craic on the bus was decent enough as it dandered back down the hill to the wheezing, bronchitic city built on the boggy Farset.

The tips weren't bad at all and Glen smiled gratefully at the Fry-boy as they all left the bus on High Street.

'God, they were mustard at the start, weren't they?' said Kenny, the driver. 'Faces on them like Lurgan spades.'

Glen laughed and made his way up to the office marked Cleary's Bus Tours. Next door was O'Hanlon's.

Inside Cleary's, John Cleary himself was standing chatting to Leanne, chinking his keys.

'Just letting you know that's me off now,' said Glen.

'What? You have a life outside here, do you?' joshed Leanne.

'Off to squander your tips down the pub, are you?' said John, the wattles on his neck blancmanging with laughter.

Glen smiled but he looked away from Leanne. A week ago, she'd caught him talking to Finn, one of O'Hanlon's crew, on the stairs. She had said nothing but he'd felt her bristle. One tour company was Prod and next door to it was Catholic and there was an invisible line between them as big as the peace wall they ferried the tourists to and from every day. It was mad, thought Glen, but the tours were of two different cities, one seen through a pair of green eyes, one through

a pair of blue. From the top of Cave Hill, you could see the white of
the peace wall trickling through the heart of the city like a line of
poisonous lime.

'That's me shooting on, peeps,' said Glen.

'And ate a fish supper!' called Leanne as he went out, making fun
of his thinness. It was all part of the slagging at Cleary's.

The room was in a top floor flat in the Markets. It was the second time
he'd donned the robes and he felt comfortable enough.

'Look up at me,' said Liam, darting his brush into the oil paint.

It was Finn who'd first approached Glen outside Cleary's. She'd
said her mate, Liam, was a painter and was looking for a model who
looked spiritual.

'Spiritual? Me?' laughed Glen. 'Sure I've never stepped foot over
a church door in years.'

'You'll get paid,' said Finn.

Liam had been commissioned privately by a priest to produce
a portrait of Jesus and he'd been well pleased to meet Glen who was
a dead ringer for God's own son with his long brown hair, gentle
eyes and thin frame. 'Imagine,' he said to Glen. 'A Catholic priest
crossing himself before you, a big bad Protestant,' and they'd gone
into wrinkles laughing at the irony of it all. Glen's mother had been
a bit of a churchgoer, a right pew-chewer as they called it, but he'd
never had much time for it himself. When he felt bad, though, he'd
still say a wee mouthful of prayer.

'Can you just put your hand up again in a blessing?' asked Liam.

Glen obliged and began to daydream, the fumes of the ochre,
cobalt blues, and the mauves and the crimsons and titanium whites
bubbling up into his brain. His eyelids slumbered. He thought of
his mother who'd died two years ago and wondered if she was up in
heaven. But when he imagined heaven, a place thronging with souls,

he knew he'd never want to go there himself. If hell was other people, then, to him, heaven was hell.

He thought of Finn and wondered why she'd come up to him that day. Was it really that she liked him? Or was it just because he was some skinny guy who would make a good Jesus? He was sure there had been warmth in her blue eyes but perhaps it had just been the sun. He remembered the way the light had cast glints on her black hair...

An hour later, he set out on the short walk home. Behind him the sun was about to set, casting a powder blue haze on the mountains before they shaded into black. A squadron of starlings surged and wheeled above the Albert Bridge against the orange-tanged sky. Turning onto the Castlereagh Road, a car tooted at him. Jimmy Rea waved and he thought, fuck, if Jimmy knew what I'd just been at, he'd go ballistic. Of course, they were used to Glen now and his oddball looks with his long 'Catholic' hair and hippy clothes, but still sometimes the locals couldn't accept that he wasn't part of the short hair, tight t-shirt brigade, the new model army of the East, where they were all churned out, identically hard as if hammered straight out of the long-defunct shipyards.

Jimmy pulled over up the road and waited for him.

'Can I bring you round a bag tonight?' he shouted out through the passenger window.

'I'm a bit busy, Jimmy, with work and all,' said Glen. 'I can't.'

'Your loss.' Jimmy drove off, his tattooed arms spinning the wheel cavalierly like it was a roulette wheel.

It had been six months since Jimmy had asked him for help. Glen had never been part of the UVF, but as Jimmy's nephew he was trusted and, as Jimmy said, he was the only person who'd count it straight. One time, he'd counted fifty-eight grand in plastic bags. He had drawn the line at stashing guns or whispering in a man's ear on the Shankill, but he had helped with the money alright. Jimmy had once bunged him five hundred quid for three hours' work.

God, it was hard to turn Jimmy down. But he had a job now, he wanted no more of that hooky stuff, every wheel and turn of it scared him now. It passed through his head that Jesus was sold for thirty pieces of silver. Thirty p, that was all. He walked on up the road, past the bright purple and orange flags of the UVF, past the pub with its CCTV camera aimed into the wall, turning a blind eye. The leaves of the trees were singed brown as if the bony arms had burnt themselves with cigarettes. Turning into his street, he could see the sun was being squeezed between the vice of cloud and hill, seemingly pinched in its anvil. He lingered on the threshold in its light before going indoors.

'I'll tear the heads off them,' said John Cleary, spitting feathers in the office.

'They're handing out leaflets on our turf, bold as you like,' explained Leanne since John was past clear articulation.

They, of course, were O'Hanlon's.

'Have you spoken to them?' asked Glen.

'There's no speaking to them lot, is there? A third we're down on bookings.'

'Sure Tuesdays are always slow,' Glen suggested quietly.

John's eyes bulged like eggs in a boiling pan. 'Well, fella, if it keeps on, you'll be crying your lamps out with the rest of us.'

Glen left hastily and ran down to the bus. As Leanne said, the numbers were low but it wasn't surprising as there was a matitudinal mizzle about and the mountains were veiled by the grey promise of more rain. He was standing waiting for the last damp stragglers when Finn walked up to him from the O'Hanlon bus.

'How's your Jesus gig going?'

Glen laughed. 'Grand. Cheers for putting it my way.'

He looked at her shyly, his hand going up to his lips as it always did when he didn't know what to say.

'Look,' said Finn, a thought brightening her eyes, 'a cuz of mine's going in for a film about the hunger strikers at Long Kesh. He's gonna starve himself to try and get a part but you'd be perfect. Why don't you go for it?'

'I don't act.'

'Sure, the spiel we do on the bus, is that not acting?'

'Aye, pretending I like the passengers, that's acting alright,' laughed Glen.

One of O'Hanlon's sales boys walked by, tossing them an odd look. They fell quiet till he'd passed.

'Sure, Glen, give it a whirl,' resumed Finn. 'Ask Liam about it.'

The bus driver revved up the engine and Glen fired a quick 'catcha' to Finn and hopped on.

The tourists were all squeezed in on the ground floor but the stairwell blew down a damp chill air as if from a chimney. Glen, warmed by meeting Finn, scarcely felt it, but still... Today the city on the Farset was cold and anonymous. Dark clumps of umbrellas mushroomed up at every street corner they passed. The traffic was slower in the rain which meant you needed more improv, more fillers. Wee joke about arranging some typical Belfast weather just for them, no extra charge.

A bored boy, Italiany-looking, kept dipping into a bag of mini-wafers. Flipped it over on his tongue, let it melt there, deliciously dissolve, like Christ's holy body dipped in sugar, before masticating the remains. For fuck sake, stop gawking at him. Europa coming up, coming up.

Not many know it, but we Belfast folk are great inventors. We actually invented the bulletproof camera which came in pretty handy when you think of it.

A couple of half-laughs bowling up from the back of the bus. Little did they know about the trouble with O'Hanlon's. He didn't want to lose this job. He was shy in real life but he'd discovered here he had a great tongue on him when called for. What other job could he get with no qualifications? At school he used to get out of class by chewing the top of the pen so the ink'd spill into his mouth. Half the time he'd looked like a Goth with black lipstick! Thinking back, it had coincided with the time he started to eat less. His mother had said nothing, but her love had been the all-colluding Belfast sort. 'Sure the sweetest meat is next to the bone,' she used to say with a grin, pinching his cheek.

As the bus turned slowly, almost reluctantly, onto the Falls, he shook away his thoughts. A billboard, 'Building a Better Belfast,' flashed up ironically in front of him.

Right, folks, we're now entering the Falls Road, famous for its Republican politics. It's also known as the Gaeltacht Quarter which along with...

The bus braked suddenly, pitching him backwards. He quickly grabbed on to a steel pole. Ffff, he said, stifling the swearwords — he was near arse over tip there! He looked round at Kenny but Kenny kept his eyes fixed on the narrow boundaries of the road and drove on.

It was Kenny's way of serving him right for his ad-lib about the Gaeltacht Quarter, for elevating the Falls into a cultural zone. Telling him to stick to his sparse script from now on. Well, at least the Italian boy was laughing away. Nothing like a near pratfall to enliven the internationals.

A few hours later, at lunchtime, the rain dribbled to a halt and the washed skies peeled away, the white sheet magically lifting from the mountainside. The hills looked freshly painted, as if on a grand unveiling.

Glen went up to the office to have his lunch. The sales boys were there and the chatter was all of O'Hanlon's tricks and what was to be done about it. They didn't spare Glen a glance and he knew they must have seen him cracking on to Finn earlier. For one terrible second he actually wondered if Finn could have been put up to it by O'Hanlon — a vision came to him of the portrait of himself as the Catholic Christ being circulated in the office, of himself on film as an IRA hunger striker. Oh, God, he'd lose his job, be shamed in the East... The sandwich in his hand was quivering and he shut it back in its box.

Stop it now, he told himself. Finn was a good girl, you could tell by the kind, open face of her. All this paranoia in the office was getting to him, that was all. He'd go for a stretch of the legs and forget about it.

'Well, at least it's brightened up,' he said to Leanne on his way out.

'That weather doesn't know what to be at,' she said coldly. 'It's neither one thing nor another.'

She was looking at him hard and he knew she was referring to him.

At five o'clock he made his way home. He passed the Albert Bridge, looking down into the bluish Lagan, prismed by the sun. A couple of old newspapers were washed up in its muddy shallows, their headlines history. Impulsively he went up the Ravenhill Road, breaking with his usual route. A few kids were kicking kerbies on a side street and the memory came back of how the kids at school used to shout, 'Bobby Sands!' at him, just because he was thin.

He decided right then to audition for the film. He wasn't going to worry about what people thought of him. He'd already freed himself from Jimmy. The flags on the lamp posts rippled at him in admonishment but he didn't care. My girlfriend, Finn, he thought with a longing. Short for Fionnuala. He remembered how she had said his name that afternoon, Glen, a murmur in her throat and her breath like the soft west wind. He passed the church at Willowfield, the cherry trees encircling it red-flamed, dancing in the breeze like joyous hellfire. He couldn't help noticing how the roots of the trees had risen up and broken through the concrete. Too big for this place, outgrowing it. Sooner or later you would have to outgrow these streets.

Just outside his house a pigeon pecked at stones, thinking they were crumbs. The stones flew up like thrown dice. For the first time in ages Glen felt hungry.

'There you go,' said John Cleary the following morning, handing him his time sheet, not looking at him.

'What?' His three and four o'clock runs were cancelled.

'Sorry, Glen. Everyone has to take a cut this week, not just you.'

'But we have to do something.'

John's big shoulders were lowered in defeat. Even his keys registered the faintest chime now.

'Maybe you should join next door. After all, you're all pally-wally with that girl,' commented Leanne tartly.

Glen opened his mouth to speak but could say nothing.

He went down to the bus. The sun was shining off the windows of the high-rise buildings, creating vast panels of light, turning Belfast into a decadent city of gold. Tiny workers hived and droned outside towers transformed into dripping honeycombs. Some leaves fell on him like party streamers but he didn't see them. He was thinking of what they could do to fight O'Hanlon's. Back in Gaelic times, it was simple. If you were wronged by a family, you'd sit outside their house on hunger strike until they righted that wrong. If they let you die of hunger, they were shamed forever. He laughed softly to himself, thinking of the hopeless ridiculousness of it all.

Raised voices floated up to him from down the street. Cleary's sales boys were having a nip at someone and there was some sort of scuffle. Glen jumped off and ran down. Sectarian epithets cracked through the air. As Glen arrived, the O'Hanlon boy was just backing off. One of the Cleary boys had a jet-white patch just above his eye from a blow. A sudden spurt of crimson appeared as though squeezed from a tube.

'You'll need stitches on that,' his friend was saying, ushering him back towards Cleary's office. The boy had his hand over his eye, but the blood was trickling through his fingers like juice from a split fruit.

Kenny was tooting the horn, so Glen raced back to the bus and jumped on. He hardly saw the passengers, the act of violence, the cruel words still pumping through him, but he managed to talk about the city as if peace was all it knew now.

Turning onto the Lower Falls, he saw the rowan berries stamped red into the pavements and the leaves whisk along as crisp as dead skin. People walked past with their heads down, their hearts as sour as crab apples. Why shouldn't both sides tell their history to the tourists? The injustice of it stung him.

Here we are on the Falls...

A blinding anger flushed through him. All he could see was their International Wall and he wanted to tear at it with his bare hands till they bled, he longed to spit on the mural of Bobby Sands, to smash his own body up against the gable bricks, right into that smiling face of the victor for there was no ideology, only hate, hate, hate, hate in this city of murdering mammy's boys, so full of flags and dead heroes it was like living in a cenotaph, no wonder they were mad and bad and crazed and the bile black as ink rose to his lips...

The tourists were all staring at him, waiting.

Kenny crossed the peace line and pulled the bus to a halt. He got out of his cabin.

'Are you okay?' he asked, looking at Glen's whitened, sickened face.

'I'm fine,' nodded Glen. 'Just a bit of travel sickness,' he said weakly to the tourists and they looked surprised that a tour guide should suffer from it.

He felt so shamed by his thoughts. He could almost imagine Liam looking through to his soul as he painted him. Some son of God he was. He felt a heaviness grow round his legs like concrete.

Ahead of him lay the wasteland, signalling the no man's land between the Falls and the Shankill, full of rusty ferns and discarded tyres.

'Let's go on,' he said to Kenny.

Later, when he went up to the office, he walked past the smashed glass in O'Hanlon's door.

'Is that our handiwork?' he asked.

John Cleary smiled, saying nothing. It was the way it worked in this country.

'It'll all be sorted in the end,' said Leanne.

In the coming nights, Glen knew there would be the soft pad of feet outside each bus depot, a gentle shearing sound and the lighting of a match. All this would happen as naturally as the seeping of the sucking bog below these streets and the drip-drip-drip of it would go on until weariness of it all brokered a truce. Even if you didn't lift a hand, you were still secretly glad that your side wouldn't let up. It was the way of it.

Glen left the office and bounced down the steps into the street, dialling a number. All around him, soft light and billowy shadows drew pictures down the sides of the buildings.

'Hello, Liam? It's Jesus here.'

Liam laughed and listened to what he had to say about the film. Glen kept close to the wall, so no one else could hear. After a while, he unconsciously moved out onto the pavement and stayed there, letting the passers-by scurry around him.

In the distance the sun was strobing light across the mountains. The whin and the heather flickered and the tourists, oblivious that for October the sun was unusually high, made their separate ways to the two buses, just glad they had the weather and hoping their guide would teach them all they'd ever need to know about Belfast.

TRAVELS ROUND A ROOM

As Gregory Morgan floated up into consciousness, a huge, racking cough took hold of him, winched up from the depths of his chest. He juddered so much, the crumples in the white sheet beneath him appeared to stretch right onto the walls, shaking the structure of the room. When at last it was over, he opened the pale flowered curtains next to his bed. The cold from the windowpane nearly induced another coughing fit.

The light had raced into the room, squatting in the centre, leaving the shadows to reside in the dusty corners. Through the window he could see the Lisburn Road and the tattoo parlour opposite, hung with photos of fleshy lumps of shoulder, pink from the pain of the needle. He blinked to rid himself of the image of a butcher's shop. By the traffic lights a queue of cars was waiting, the faces behind dark panes pale and motionless in their heated vivariums. Gregory checked his alarm clock. It was four in the afternoon. A great splash fell onto the pavement below, exploding into a silver star, and soon the window itself was wreathed with falling smiles of rain. Gregory noticed suddenly how the white sky blanched out the harshness in people's faces, illuminating their youth. It was a miserable, pissing-down day, Ireland was just a big sponge, as everyone said, and yet Gregory was blissfully happy.

Gregory knew his own condition. It was anhedonia, defined in the dictionary as, 'inability to feel pleasure in normally pleasurable activities'. Well, it wasn't a total inability as much as a reduced capacity. That was the trouble with self-diagnosis, it could never be one hundred per cent accurate. Sometimes, he blamed the way he was on his low blood pressure. 'It makes you feel tired, lethargic, dizzy, doesn't it?' the doctor had said to him years before, lingering over the symptoms like a clairvoyant making a meal of a great revelation. In his normal state, Gregory felt himself to be dull (to give an indication of that dullness, he was a civil servant who'd never once called in sick) and that was why he'd decided to devote this year to finding the adrenalin points, to finding out what really made him buzz.

He pulled the duvet down, letting the cold air of the room rest like fog on the warm sweat of his chest. It was going to be a difficult balance—he didn't want to go too far but he had to find a way of maintaining this level of illness.

A light tap sounded, so cautious that Gregory wondered what it was, then realised it came from the cheap egg-box door of his own room.

'Gregory,' said a voice—it belonged to his housemate, Emmet. 'Gregory,' it said, more loudly. 'Are you okay?'

Gregory sat up with a start, fearing Emmet might burst in, before remembering that the door automatically locked when you shut it. He had a further shock as he heard his own voice answer, accompanied by a hacking cough that rose up, reverberating around the words, drowning them out entirely. 'I'm quite okay,' he tried to say again with the same noisy result.

When the coughing fit had stopped, he could hear a low exchange of words from the landing between Emmet and one of the other housemates. He couldn't hear what they were saying but he frowned.

Certainly he wasn't sure how many days he'd stayed alone in this room but he wouldn't have put it at more than four and, besides, had he ever passed comment on Emmet's habit of coming home rat-arsed and flaking out on the sofa after waking everyone up with ham-fisted attempts to put the key in the lock? 'Do I ever interrupt you when you're lying pissed in your room?' Gregory would have liked to know.

The voices faded as footsteps padded down the stairs, but Gregory kept his ears pricked just in case. After a minute, he relaxed, noticing in the slight steam emanating from his body's contact with the cold air that the dark hairs looked like a series of notes, of crotchets, minims and quavers beginning to dance along the white page of his chest.

He wondered how bad he looked so he craned his head out of the bed until he could see his reflection in a long section of mirror attached to the wardrobe. He hardly recognised that figure; those bright piercing eyes of a prophet, the white-flecked creviced lips like the cliffs of a promontory. By rights, this stranger should have alarmed him but he was no longer sure if he could depend upon his eyes as reliable guides to the truth.

It all began to flood back to him, the first leg of that year's adventure, the beginning of drug-taking that had opened up new vistas, new trajectories of thinking that had fluted his mind into paeans of sheer pleasure. It had given him highs he'd never known existed, first passing through the tingling brainwash of a starry sea, loosening his brain to the moving motes in every object, thumb-printing his eyes with their traducing beauty, adding layer upon layer with the tip of a pointillist's brush. Those pills and powders and herbs had nailed a gallimaufry of boneless puppets to the walls, dancing and feverishly shaking, while their full-blooded counterparts drifted slowly, their bodies swimming through a communal tide as their brains kept crashing on the same shore. And just when he thought he could go no higher, he'd run outside and throw himself on the ground, looking up at the golden pollen in the black bloom of the sky.

It didn't take him long to discover that it was impossible to recreate. Weeks passed of intensifying the doses and yet he never could approach the same heights. He looked around at the addicts, the need tethered on their hollow faces, and he realised that they devoted their lives to hope, soaring the same contrails in the sky, following the same boring stratospheric paths, then sliding back down, hauling their shelled-out skulls painfully across the earth. He was tired of feeling like a car someone had joyridden and left burnt out at the side of the road. Thankfully he found himself able to walk away, thinner, intense-eyed, but without suffering too heavy a toll on his health.

He nodded to himself as though listening to a story told by a friend. He felt the slow creep of pins and needles in his nose and he reached across to the bedside table for a handkerchief. The white light from the window had chalked his room into relief. Clothes that had been hastily discarded lay everywhere, sometimes reclining with the semblance of bodies in chilled-out poses. It was a mess but there was never enough storage space in rented rooms.

After experimenting with drugs, he'd felt depressed — not enough to take time off from the Civil Service but he realised that the only cure was to find the next buzz. As it happened, a friend invited him to a church group. He'd never really been into recreational religion but found himself fascinated, inspired even, to know that Jesus hadn't been about rules, but freedom from rules. On one Saturday afternoon in a church hall, his friends invited the Holy Spirit to join them and his heart began to beat, to flap with a million wings. It was like *The Bible* was a pill he had swallowed whole and the words were showering through his soul, the significance of that moment reaching right down into the root of his life. Going home, his heart was bursting like a pod with seeds of goodness and along the streets cherry blossom bubbled and frothed on the branches as if filled with the same impulse.

The trouble was, he'd never been able to recreate that moment. Sometimes he'd be pulled into the vivifying words of *The Bible* only to be raised midway and dropped.

A loud knock came from the front door. Gregory wondered which of the housemates it could be. They were always forgetting their keys. Even worse, Emmet would go to the shops, leaving the front door wide open to the beasts and burglars of the day.

He turned round in his bed and pushed his face up to the window. No, whoever it was, they were sheltering from the rain, standing so close to the door he couldn't see them. Between the brick wall and the windowsill a spider's web glimmered with beads of rain no bigger than pinheads, shining among the black tracery like a constellation map. To the side of the window was the black-soaked tree with roots that had swollen the pavement into waves and were almost breaking through the flagstones. The past two years he'd lived in this room, he had felt a special affinity with this tree, as if he too was encased in circumstances, unable to break free.

Unsatisfied with drugs and religion, he'd immersed himself in a new passion: going to meetings against the state and hanging out with anarchists and socialists whose minds had been branded at impressionable ages with the white heat of ideologies. The demos had hooked him further, the chants, the euphoria, the primitive beat of the samba drums; it had felt to him like the dawn of civilisation, a protean world of possibility. He craved further fixes so he took his annual leave in the great battlegrounds of international summits where he locked arms with thousands. It seemed to him that his whole existence was a frame for that moment, a conduit through which the love and the hate of the group could freely course. His body was no more than a banner of protest, he had no mind, no self and he existed as pure breath. He almost wept to relive such perfect freedom.

A brisk rap sounded on his door. 'Gregory, Gregory.'

This time Gregory was incensed. 'Go away, will you?' he called but the choking cough took away the distinctness of each word.

'Gregory, someone's here to see you.' Emmet spoke emphatically as though to someone with head trauma. 'Listen, if you don't open the door, I'm going to force it open.'

And who's going to pay for the new lock, thought Gregory

angrily. He rolled his feet to the edge of the bed, wriggling them out from under the duvet which felt incredibly heavy. His feet, he noticed, were so thin, the tendons stood up on ridges attached to each toe, like an athlete's feet which had been in hard training for months. He was about to try to sit up upright when the door snapped open, a piece of the lock firing across the room and hitting the wall.

Emmet's face and that of a woman appeared from around the door.

'That will be eight pounds seventy, please,' said Gregory.

Oh, he couldn't get over Emmet playing the responsible house-mate, playing night nurse. Oh, just you wait, the next time you're lying comatose with the drink we'll get an ambulance for you and see how you like it. Do you know, Gregory wanted to say to the woman, this is the pillock drinks himself incontinent, the traces are everywhere, so whatever you do, don't sit on our sofa.

Emmet's mouth lengthened as he surveyed Gregory and he drew back slowly as if pushed back by some steady invisible force. Perhaps the room stinks, thought Gregory in embarrassment. Four days and no air. If only he could have reached up beforehand to open the window.

The woman was holding a black clipboard tight to her heart like a shield. She looked vaguely familiar to him but he couldn't think from where. She stepped carefully over the strewn floor although she was clearly a woman who would have preferred to charge forward. To Gregory it seemed that an element of nature was entering the dingy room, her face flushed from the fresh air, her brown hair streaming back from her face like wind-driven branches, thickets of eyelashes spiking around dark mottled irises. He could even make out a shadow in the white of her throat like the vein of a leaf, spreading little tributaries of movement through the muscles and tendons of her face. And yet all this wildness was contained in a dark, sober suit. On closer examination her suit and thinly plucked eyebrows implied that she was someone of a tidy, geometrical mind.

'Gregory Morgan?' she checked.

For one second Gregory wriggled over to the wall thinking she was about to sit on the side of the bed but she pulled up a chair.

'I'm from the fifth floor of the Agency.'

He shrank back, remembering he'd heard of such check-ups. The swirl of the room had suddenly been sucked up into her black pupils fixed as nail heads. He hadn't felt the jolt of reality in days and it came as a shock.

'I've been charged with the not very pleasant task,' she paused for no more than a second, her eyes rolling round the room to leave Gregory in no doubt she found herself in an invidious environment, 'of finding out what's become of you. You have been absent for a total of four days and on no occasion did you call in, phone in, email, fax or text us to explain yourself. It's all very unsatisfactory.'

Gregory cringed, recalling the rulebook. How could it be that he had completely forgotten about work? Had he been so caught up in himself?

'Fair enough, you haven't been a bad worker, it's true,' she allowed, 'but there are concerns about certain eccentricities — your anti-corporate tendencies, shall we say.' She looked at him out of the corner of her eyes. 'I should warn you it takes very little to turn what has been a Cause for Concern into a Cause for Dismissal.'

He sat up, alarmed. 'But everything I've been into, I've done outside work. I would never compromise the office.'

'Gregory, Gregory.' She had put up her finger to silence him. It stood in the air like an exclamation mark. 'Hear me out, please. There are rumblings that you've been taking time off to further your extra-curricular career. On Tuesday,' she consulted the clipboard, 'you were allegedly seen on TV demonstrating in the West Bank. The most serious accusation occurred yesterday when you were reported snorting cocaine on a church altar in Sligo.'

'That's mad in the head!' exploded Gregory. 'Can't you see I'm in bed?'

'Well, I can only discount these theories if I know what is wrong with you.'

Gregory began to tell her about his illness, describing the weight-lessness and heaviness that kept swaying within him, the tingle in his gums, the tightness in his nostrils, the crackling in his throat that gave way to the hot stipple of sensation running down the inside of his chest, the feel of the skin retracting around his cheekbones, the static buzz around his head like he was wearing a phantom hat, the riffs running right through his body, and he realised as he described his senses that the pleasure far outweighed the pain of his illness and that once more he had found a way to feel alive. It was yet another metamorphosis of feeling.

'You have a cold,' said the woman dispassionately. 'Listen, Gregory, the rest of us turn up for work unless we're on our deathbeds. We can't have this at all, you in your own rarified little world, not caring a thing about your colleagues. And look at you, you haven't shaved in days. Letting yourself go like this,' she said reproachfully, rolling over his attempts to speak. 'Don't try to turn me. Believe me, I can hear the grass grow a mile away. It's the height of self-indulgence to make me travel all the way out to see you and on such a miserable day too.'

Gregory turned. It had darkened and the rain fell in a white rush from the bright weirs of streetlights, scattering a foamy light through the branches of trees onto the faces of passers-by. The guttering along the roofs of shops was open-jawed, raindrops suspended like grinning white teeth set in mossy gums. The scene was so beautiful it stirred in his chest, opening out within the intractably tight space like the unfurling petals of a giant flower and he fell into a long coughing fit.

'You haven't been looking after yourself, Gregory. Not looking after your body, over-feeding your mind.'

'Look, I'm sorry. I'll go back to work first thing on Monday.' He raised his voice, deciding to put her straight. 'But hang on here a sec — if you looked at my records you'd see I've never taken a sickie in my life.'

The arch of the plucked eyebrows was repeated in the wrinkles of the astonished forehead.

'Past records cut no ice with us. It's governmental policy. I thought you'd read the white paper. You're only as good as your last day. Everyone in your department signed to say they'd read the white paper, but I can see you cut corners and didn't even give it a glance. Here's me giving you a window of opportunity and what do you do but throw it back at me. Return to work on Monday? Any employee worth their salt would come back tomorrow.' She sprang to her feet. 'No, really we're going to have to take the matter into our own hands to get you up and about. This is for your own good, Gregory.'

She launched herself at the duvet, grabbing it off him. His hands seemed to move after it in slow motion but it was too late. She stared at his naked body, clasping the great mass of duvet to her own body almost in protection.

'I'm sorry. I had no idea,' she murmured, aghast.

Gregory pulled back the duvet from her and covered himself, cowering in his bed. He'd never been more embarrassed in his life.

'You're very, very ill,' said the woman, turning away from him. 'Clearly very ill,' she repeated, leaving the room with an exaggeratedly soft tread as though leaving the room of someone who was sleeping.

Gregory was dismayed. He pulled up the duvet and checked himself. He didn't think his manhood was sufficiently repellent to provoke such a response. 'Most unsatisfactory,' he said to himself, unconsciously mimicking the speech of the woman.

Very slowly Gregory eased himself out of bed. He put on his dressing gown with difficulty. His whole back was hunched and aching. The yellow carpet lit up like sun on dry grass and he banished the image, pulling tight on the tourniquet inside his mind. He pulled himself up straight, like a confirmation of new intentions.

Now she'd put the idea into his head, he was looking forward to working again; the predictable normality of the office would be like balm to his soul. He imagined himself back at his desk, immersed in the tap of computer, the familiar fisk of paper. He remembered the calm airiness of the office, though, of course, he corrected himself harshly, there could be tension too. Suddenly, he could feel the boss's mind, stepping into the elevator of a great idea, born away to the upper heavens of the fifth floor; he could hear the urgent cluck of the mail in the rattling pigeonholes, he could almost see the mainframe computer next to his seat, the coloured lights in the plastic box dancing, sonically pulsing, dilating like drugged pupils, maddened motes and the rows of faces illuminated by the bright work-screens, a fevered light that inspired, a deliverance, a messianic radiance. Could it be, could it just be, he questioned, quelling the coughs on the sleeve of his dressing gown, that the idea of work excites me?

VALERI

For the past hours I haven't been able to sleep. There is a charged atmosphere in the dark of my room, communicated by the frenzied painting carried out by the Russian artist who rents the room next door. The thin wall fairly vibrates with it. There are coughs and imprecations, lovers' words and sighs, monologues splitting into dialogues of differing views, becoming more and more impassioned. Oh, yes, and the clinks of the vodka bottle.

I don't see much of Valeri but I do know that by day he briefly leaves the intoxicating upper realms of the first floor to wander our shared living room in a state of fugue and to scavenge from our fridge. I think he should eat more. He seems to have the idea that food interferes with the artistic process, weighing you down, whereas a heavy bladder and semi-inebriation don't seem to pose a problem.

My eyes keep springing open on gusts of thought. My room is a dark landscape with a white shadowy sky; the wardrobe stands like a distant skyscraper and beyond the curtains lies a similar terrain surmounted by moonlit clouds. You can make out the backyards and alleyways and the shining teeth of barbed wire which resemble the cluttered path to the door of my own room. It's mad but the symmetry is mind-blowing.

Mutterings come louder than ever from next door. His words spray abrasively like the sand from the gritters that roll round our frozen streets. He's really starting to unnerve me, so I break my policy of no interference, switch on the bedside lamp and get up, slipping my arms into my dressing gown.

I'm surprised to see Valeri's door ajar, like an open hand extending an invitation. He's at his easel drawing frenziedly with pastels, the air a sandstorm of reds and oranges around him. His white-blond hair, tied back into a tight bud by day, has been let loose and smothers his face. Crouched on a ramskin that covers the seat of the wooden chair, he attacks the paper, his long toes curling over the chair's edge. He's naked but for a pair of white briefs.

His head swings round to me. The combination of flared nostrils, staring eyes and fluid frown is bizarrely compelling.

'Come in, come in. I need you to tell me what you think. No, not this,' he says impatiently, ripping the pastel picture off the easel. He pulls me over to the table through the iridescent air, shimmering with powdery colour.

'This.'

This is an oil painting of a woman lying at the base of a weeping willow. The long, languid branches rustle erotically over her nudity. And suddenly I'm so close I can feel the hurl of blossoms and seeds in the hot breeze. It's incredible — the lustre of new greenery foams from every treetop and I'm almost jealous of her spot on that soft bed of yellow catkins. The tips of the branches are a thousand needles of a compass, febrile, sensitive, moving across the map of her body.

He's unbelievably tense. Dominating his face is a fine nose with large, chiselled nostrils like those of an overbred racehorse. His face quivers, awaiting my verdict.

'Have you ever made love with a tree?'

I laugh out loud. 'What do you mean by that?'

His turquoise eyes frown at me. His face has a shifting landscape of furrows and channels, pools and clefts that keep you fascinated. 'I mean with the branch of a willow.'

I'm about to laugh again but I stop, remembering a feeling years before about the pink, round-headed buds of the rhododendron in our garden, sprouting like pubescent penis heads, and how one beautiful May night I had leant down to kiss one.

'Well, there was a rhododendron bush,' I confess.

He smiles with a long lip that pulls down over his top teeth like a blind. The whole effect is lazily attractive.

He leads me by the hand and sits me down on the edge of his bed. The duvet lies in a swirl like piped icing, a meringue confection of marshmallow softness and he smooths it out behind me. He pours vodka into two glasses and we bolt it down as though it's a pact. His hand grazes his stomach thoughtfully. I find him totally mesmerising.

'You seem stressed,' he says, going down on one knee and pulling off my left shoe. 'I want to care for you a little.'

He massages my foot, gently at first, then digs his thumbs so hard into the ball of my foot that I squeal.

'Don't move. Relax,' he says. He has a wicked grin on his face and my whole body has come alive. The easel looks like a religious cross against the dismal curtains.

'Go back to work, you sadist,' I tell him but he smiles and bends over, kissing my ankle softly with his lips, all the while looking up at me.

'I won't hurt you again,' he whispers and he caresses my foot, making soft noises in his throat as a child would with a much-loved animal.

The skin on his face is badly pitted but its dazzling white blinds you to the blemishes. On his upper arm he has a white tattoo of a dragon which is hidden in the lair of his own pallor. He's wiry and well-made and the shadows follow the line of his muscled skin; the contrast is like snow on the bark of a tree. He smiles seductively as he pulls the other shoe from my foot. He squeezes the leather as though popping a seed from its pod.

I lie back waiting for his enfolding hands but nothing happens. He's deep in thought with my shoe in his hand, looking at it meditatively.

'This is the answer. A shoe lying in the forest like a conch... It lies there... a black spyhole, to show how dark the night can be...'

He lifts up the shoe as he speaks, as if to put his lips to the dark neck of the opening, running his hands over the sole, bending the soft leather.

'No, can't you see it as a hollow in the tree? No, even better a symbol of feminine wounds, and behind it the pink buds of the rhododendron sway...'

'What are you doing with my shoe, Valeri?'

But he's moving quickly towards the easel, flinging another piece of paper into its spindly arms. He sets the shoe on the table and begins to paint, his nostrils shivering as though inhaling the freshness of spring flowers. The tip of the brush flits across the page with the zip of a dragonfly skimming a pond.

He shakes his hair out of his eyes. He once told me his fingers turned black with frostbite in a Russian army jail, so he has to paint fast now. His movements speed up, his hands dart with the poesy of revolution, his paintbrush clouding the jar of water with tints of storm and sunset, making a breach against the empty Belfast winter that's sapped our senses with a chiaroscuro of white rain-splashes and the black of long nights.

Valeri fences at the paper, his eyes ablaze, full of shiny blue iris. It seems he has hardly any whites to his eyes and they've gone huge like wrap-around sunglasses. He snatches open the curtains to let the sky see his work. His head twitches as the brushstrokes circle furiously and his body curves, bright and hard like a white salamander. Am I crazy or is it really him shooting in a zigzag of light against the dark windowpane? One thing is sure, I'm outstaying my welcome and I leave quietly—but not before out the corner of my eye I catch him undulating violently, his body now flat and reptilian, all the hot blood of his creativity spent on the painting, as he battles on against the boredom of the night.

Back in my room again, my eyes adjust to the darkness, translating its shapes and shadows. Outside the window an estuary of light briefly trickles down through the cloud dams and bottle-necks into a moon-soaked lake on a rooftop. The light reflects onto my ceiling in a translucent pool and then it's gone. When I look up, stars sparkle in the blackness as does the ice below in the alleys. Suddenly every image around me is part of one big continuum. The floral pattern on my curtain sways darkly, just as outside the moving print of bare branches is cast onto the grey leaf of open pavement.

I hug myself on my bed, half out of my head from reliving Valeri's touch. Perhaps I could go back to him later for my shoe, but... no. There's only one thing to do now and I take off my dressing gown. Then I slowly lie back on top of the bedcovers, the painting in my mind, letting the boughs of flickering shadows blow across my body.

APPOINTMENT

Everyone knows how easy it is to be late. Time has a habit of operating in fits and starts; it comes in seasons, short or lengthy, sprouting strange lacunae like pages torn from a calendar. Drop your guard for an instant and time will leapfrog forward in mad multiples when all morning you've been lulled by its lagging moratoriums.

Yesterday morning, time hung loosely and I lost control. Not that it was my fault for being late. Why do we even try to harness nature mathematically, when there are so many freaks of growth like a Leap Year Day or a half-witted flower coming out in winter?

Going back to yesterday, I was getting ready in the bathroom when I was distracted by the shell-whorl of water slewing into the basin. It was only for a moment but time took advantage and, before I knew it, I was really running late for my appointment. The pigeons on the outside eaves were flapping their wings like harshly turned pages in a book, telling me to quicken up. I turned off the taps, drying my hands. The plughole was sucking the water with greedy enjoyment, a glottal stop of fulfilment issuing from the silvery larynx and, when I looked down, the last beads of water winked a quick goodbye.

Dad was in his armchair, deeply embedded in its calyx, his bare feet petal-pink in their slippers, his fingers scuttering along his scalp, lifting his nebulous hair like the wind. For some time now I'd been concerned that Dad had been suffering from an excess of time leading to an obsessional interest in the weather. Once an active seaman, he was now housebound, reluctantly swapping the cirrocumuli, altostrati and nimbuses dancing in the sky for the solid white ceiling of the living room. It wasn't a healthy state of affairs although I let him get on with it. He seemed content enough. In the cyclonic gloom of our living room he was watching the weather, staring at the TV through eyes the misted blue of bilberries, as he once used to watch Sirius from the ship's wheelhouse, navigating the night seas by its light, trusting in the message of clouds.

'Hurry up. Don't waste the weather,' he called to me without moving his gaze from the screen. 'You'll need your umbrella just in case,' he reminded, while a sudden glint of sunlight through the window cheekily answered him back.

Outside, bright eyelashes of sun were bursting through rain-clouds. The last umbrellas disappeared into bags, rain glimmering on their dark material like a constellation. The air was strumming with warmth and dissolving rain. Soon there was a peppery fire to the day, the pavement billowing with powdery spirals and dessicated remains of old leaves, a Bombay orange spicing the coolest of shadows. When I reached the Lisburn Road, the bus was pulling away from its stop and I made a forlorn dash for it but it was hopeless. It was a purely symbolic effort, a piqued rail against time itself.

The truth is that nothing can be on time without sheer good fortune. There are always shunts and stalls of time and even the bus drivers know that the notion of a schedule is a man-made vagary. I checked my watch, going, 'fuck it, fuck it,' knowing I was going to be so late, trying to keep an eye out for the next bus but yesterday was one of those days when it was too easy to be sidetracked by the garrulity of nature. Birdsong soared like one of life's sweet pinches on the soul and everywhere voices hatched and trembled under resonant skies.

A bus came out of nowhere and was about to fly contemptuously past, when I flagged it down. Just in time! I took a seat on the upper deck. From our high-up perch, we passed vast swards of green-mildewed roofs and vivid tribal flags lit by the sun and in the distance yellow cranes were pulling tall edifices up like a stack of cards under a magician's wand. Branches sucked clean, their tips manicured by the winter, were clattering against the windows. In every side street people were emerging from their houses, the pinky-white blossom of fresh air blooming in their cheeks.

Passengers came on with a blast of cold air, dispersing into the discernible smells of sour alcohol, musky pheromones, perfumed powderiness and damp clothes beginning to smoke in the sun. Two girls sat down in front of me, their Belfast accents cracking out words like hot slack from a coal fire. The sharp peaks of their lips mirrored the hard flair of their nostrils, the chewing of gum quivering through their jaws like wind-flaws on water. I watched as one girl, with two palms closed votively up to her lips in bouts of amused horror, told stories to her friend whose hand had moved up to her ear as though wanting to block out the words, while at the same time her little finger extended towards the corner of her mouth, touching the bottom lip compulsively, sensuously. It was clear that tales of a sexual nature were being decanted in those deep whispers. I found myself drawn into the shiver of one earring, a little mirror suspended on a chain, swinging and circling gyroscopically, a metre of time constantly ticking. It reminded me to check my watch and time had surged forward once again in a sudden burst like a teenager's spurt of growth.

Fortunately we were nearing the city centre now, taxis scuttling out of littered streets like black rats, the pavements punctuated with puddles of shattered glass where car windows had been put out with claw hammers. As we passed the famous Crown Bar, doormen in black overcoats hawked onto the step and flexed their muscles, pressing their thumbs into the fleshy pads at the stem of each finger. Hardmen walked with strength in their swaying shoulders, the gold coins on their chains oscillating with each brisk, tight step and I hurried downstairs so I'd be the first to get off the bus.

It was a relief to hear my feet click onto the pavement. The sun was lasering itself through the tall buildings, blasting the final impurities from the blue sky. The clouds had almost gone and I was on a high. I could see the contrails of an airplane like a long line of pure cocaine chopped up by a razor and I felt that if I raised my nostrils I could sniff it up at one swoop. But I was still anxious about being late and I pressed forward into the welts of darkness cast by the buildings. I was angry to notice that yet another Victorian house had been sliced off a row, revealing an old chimney like a spine, butchered, its neighbours slumped ever more despondently beneath the towering shopping centres.

I was borne up in dark floes of people clouding the pale pavements and, beneath me, shoe prints wet from sporadic puddles ran forth like waving ferns or little darting tribes of trilobites. I headed up towards St Mary's with its holy trinity of pub, chapel and bookie's, the street littered with the crumpled dreams of discarded betting slips. Behind the grilled windows lining The Hercules Bar, I caught sight of a girl's breasts like white pickles pressing up against the side of the jar in the brown-vinegar of the interior. The old door tilted somnolently, the door jamb and lintel a clumsy dolmen through which drinkers stumbled, faces snagging and laddering on the sharp needle of daylight. Up ahead a man was holding a can, manoeuvring socially between passers-by. It was as if he was at a cocktail party on the swaying deck of a ship.

'Did I not use to go with you?' he called out hopefully to a beautiful girl, humour crumbling his oaten face. 'It was a long time ago now.'

Beside him loitered a grisaille of hardened drinkers, wearing stupefied grey masks, their tongues clotted and clogged with bitten-off words, sleeved in beer up to their elbows. They moved with raised hoofs through imaginary tussocks, their bovine faces chewing on the cud of the day's beers. Next to their dullness, the man shone with the golden face of a life spent in the open air, the sun blonding the crimped seedheads of his hair, wild sideburns winging either side of his jaw. A sprinkling of yellowish marram grass grew from the sands of his chin.

The man eyed me up, shifted as though to tackle me mid-step. From his lips I heard the click and the whoo of cigarette exhalation.

'You wouldn't spare a bit of change, darlin', would you?'

I laughed at the beer can sitting in his hand like a collection box and he drew his lips down in mirrored amusement, sucking in his cheeks and rolling his eyes. I walked on, winding my speed down and down, looking back at him. He was still smiling mischievously at people, the leaves scurrying round his feet, performing triple Salchows and curveting joyously, throwing themselves into the fun. I felt a grin tugging on my lips and suddenly I realised that I had made my appointment just in time. For years I had been searching for visual music in the great fugue of life and at last yesterday I'd found it again! I'd never forgotten that dawn walking home in the fog, witnessing the perfect note of a hook-shaped tree trunk standing behind a park bench, suspended stark, midrib the white, a crotchet inscribed onto the bars on a page. Wasn't that exact same note there in the dirt and freckles between the lines of his forehead? A musical script, stirred by the wind, peeling back page after page of harmonies, riffed with life experience. It was the only appointment worth recognising in a money-mad world. Moments like this kept dissolving into blue silence just to return on the chime of a happy mood weeks or years later.

I made my way back to the bus stop, the light guttering through the dark moraine of the streets as the sun started to sink, dipping taut bright lines into the earth. I said goodbye to the city lights, bulbous as frogspawn in the fading afternoon.

In the house, Dad was still sitting in his chair but he had lapsed into a reverie, his eyes glazed, protruding, enamelled. The twenty-four-hour weather channel was progressively taking on a hysterical tone with its isobars and turbulent depression and wild weather warnings.

'Don't you be going out tonight,' he said to me, his eyes flaring with fear. 'There's a hell of a bad storm brewing.'

Though he normally hung on every word of the weather report, tonight the muscles in his face were as tense as a butcher's slicing wire. The hair on his head and arms stood up on end like a breathing hybrid of fur from every animal: fox, wolf and bear, all matted and hot from the chase. He was more nervous than I'd ever seen.

I watched on in a kind of horror as the black lines across the country curved and tightened, sucking the diagrams of clouds and raindrops into its maelstrom of darkness. The screen fuzzed into a black and white storm and, incredibly, the first snowflakes spun out in a roar of wind from its depths, spits of howling white drowning me out. I couldn't believe what was happening!

The room tilted in the grip of a seething storm and I clung to the radiator, crying out to Dad to be careful but the last sight I had of him was his face grinning and turning in the fury of the wind, his hair a wild coil, holding up his hand in a salute. A sudden rattle of hail blasted through the room and his lips traced the final words of an old sailor's incantation as he flew up on his armchair through the shattered window. With a subsiding whistle the snow fell back gently on the carpet, onto the dusty gap where Dad's chair had sat for years.

'Dad! Dad!' I shouted as I ran outside, yelling into the sky where the pink moon calmly reflected the sunset. There was no sign of him, no reply.

Neither the chair nor Dad returned last night but I haven't given up hope. All I know is that this final rudderless journey must have taken place in some strange quirk of time, a chimerical blip mimicking the swirl of the weather. In spite of my sadness, I might as well console myself that it was high time he left the confines of the room. Dad's whereabouts may be impossible to forecast but last night I dreamt I heard him chuckling as he steadily navigated the vast waters around the stars. A man with the salt sea in his veins could hardly be expected to settle down forever.

THE HEALING FIELD

There was a great turnout for Hughie Glass at the hotel. Now that Hughie had been buried, the air was full of craic as old friends were reunited. There was talk from his cousins of what a good funeral package the hotel had put together and, seeing how the weather was, they were glad they'd gone for the deal with the hot sausage rolls and bowls of chips rather than just the sandwiches.

'Awful sorry about the rain though,' said Hughie's sister to Erwin White, who smiled to himself as he knew she always took it personally when the sun didn't shine on her gatherings. All around Erwin, people were post-morteming the funeral and saying how much they'd appreciated the readings and tributes. It seemed that everyone was talking in order to block out one thing: the horrifying way in which Hughie had died.

Erwin looked round the room for Martha. She was offering around the tray bakes, while occasionally popping one into her own mouth. It was well her mouth was full, thought Erwin, to keep her from talking. You had to be at her all the time — Judith had warned him to watch her. At a previous gathering Martha had announced to everyone that she loved Sinn Fein's Gerry Adams, an opinion that didn't go down well with the Protestant community of Armagh at the best of times. But on the day of Hughie's funeral, it would have been unthinkable.

'To one of the best men God ever pumped breath into,' said Hughie's cousin, making a toast at the bar. 'To Hughie,' chorused a few of the men, drinking, and the cousin joked, 'What's the difference between an Irish wedding and a funeral…? One less drunk!' The truth was, as Erwin knew well, Hughie had been a right sobersides, had hardly touched a drop, but everyone let it pass, just grateful for the lightness. Hughie's son, who'd returned from Leeds for the funeral, was chatting to a couple of the farmers about land and the chances of a quick sale, while his mother stood next to them, bereft.

An hour later, Erwin and Martha drove home through the wet, Martha clutching a paper plate of tinfoiled buns that slithered across her lap at every winding corner. He knew it would cowp but he didn't have the energy to argue with her today.

'That was some craic, wasn't it, Daddy?'

'Sad though that Hughie was laid to rest.'

'I'm not sad,' said Martha. 'Sure he never liked me anyway.'

He glanced across at her, taking in the familiar set of her fleshy face, its toothy grin, the eyes moving about unfixed like loose grey bolts. Often he wondered what went on in that head of hers and he couldn't fathom out why she loved some people to death but would take against others eternally, for no apparent reason. He'd always tried to avoid thinking what would become of her if he or Judith went, but, on the day of Hughie's funeral, it couldn't help but be in his mind. It was just as well that his son, James, was off in Australia, on the tail-end of his year out, travelling and working round sheep farms. Erwin had never been to Australia himself, but the country conjured up shards of flitting light and heat and he drove on almost blinded by his imagination.

He pulled the car into the old farmyard. The wind was whipping the drizzle across the gravel in pale translucent waves that looked like dust swirls. Martha squealed as she and her buns made a run for it to the door.

'Feeling any better?' he asked Judith who was ironing in the kitchen.

Judith shook her head, her lips pursed. Whenever she pursed her lips, he noticed the wrinkles. She was fifty-four, one year younger than himself, though, to be fair, she looked younger. He, on the other hand, had always looked older than he was. His skin was as deeply pitted round his jaw as cattle hooves in the clay.

'So who all was there?' Judith wanted to know.

He ran through the names of the local families: the McMullans, the Lindsays, the Millses, Mr Suchenabody… He didn't want to talk about it. Martha brought in some wood for the fire.

'At least if you two die, we've enough wood for your coffins,' she said with a grin.

'Martha!' snapped Judith. 'I hope you didn't say anything like that to Hughie's wife.'

'No, no, she was good,' said Erwin, keeping the peace and not wanting to admit he hadn't kept tabs on Martha all day. He settled the wood into the fireplace. Behind him, he could hear the creaks of the ironing board. It had never occurred to him before but it sounded like the creaks of their bed during sex.

Martha picked up her wool and needles. She was knitting jackets for orphans in Eastern Europe. Every so often Judith would check up on her because of the incident a year back when Martha had knit Gerry Adams one of those cable-knit jumpers he appeared so fond of. Martha had sent it off to him in a package, marked 'Gerry Adams, Belfast' with an invitation to come to their farm for tea. The first Judith and Erwin knew of it was a letter from one of Adams' PAs thanking Martha for her very kind offer and how, although the peace process had enabled Gerry to travel far and wide through Ireland, he would have to decline. Judith had shouted at Martha for a full day but Martha had decided that Gerry was one of the people she loved in this world, and wouldn't be budged.

'I think I'll go up and have a wee lie-down,' said Judith, setting down the iron. 'The head's dinging.'

'Take the feverfew,' he said, but she didn't acknowledge it.

He wondered if she was punishing him. After what had happened to Hughie, she'd maybe expected an immediate decision to leave the farm. He'd told her at the time not to worry, had laughed it off with a bit of bravado, 'Sure, me, I'll live so long I'll make Methuselah look like a boy.' It was true that since Brexit the border had hardened and trouble was spreading, but hadn't they stayed on their land all through the Troubles? Wasn't it only a one-off because Hughie had been kicking up a shindy about that parade?

She'd always been prone to headaches. She was so fragile it was no wonder she'd had difficulty having kids. Though to be fair they'd never been checked out and perhaps he was faulty down there too. After three miscarriages, she'd finally had Martha at the age of thirty-two. Martha had nearly died twice at birth but by some miracle survived. The doctors had said she'd never be able to talk or do anything for herself, but she'd proved them all wrong. Then, four years after, came the unexpected arrival of James, perfectly healthy and born with big farmers' hands like his father and limbs as long as a foal's.

An hour later, there was a partition in the skies and the grey curtains of cloud rolled back to reveal a pale blue window. Erwin pulled his boots on and headed out into the yard. The rainwater was gushing down to the drains in weaving plaits and the world felt fresh and clean. He decided to check up on the newly planted trees in the orchard. As he walked, he realized he'd never again see the sight of Hughie Glass on the brow of the nearby hill, coming down through the hollow, swinging his shoulders. Well, there was no point in thinking about it — the whole countryside was changing. There was the fella with the polytunnels of marijuana on his acre of land and the police never batted an eye at it.

A bird cracked a twig in the hedgerow and he swung round.

Now he was far from the house, he realized he was breathing a little faster. He looked up at the sky, reassured by its evening softness, a few strands of grey straggling across its pallor like the combover of an elderly man. Everything was fine, he told himself. That was until he reached the orchard and saw for himself.

That night he awoke as if to a phantom gunshot. His whole body was straining. He'd been dreaming that dream again. The one about the sow. The story his father had once told him about a young farmer's wife who'd left the pram with her newborn baby outside for some air. When she came back out again she discovered that a sow had knocked the pram over and eaten her baby. At intervals through his life, the events kept coming back to him in a nightmare. 'Old people dream dreams, young people see visions,' he said to himself, wondering where he'd learnt the quote.

Judith stirred next to him. She wasn't sleeping well herself since Hughie Glass's murder a month ago. He checked the alarm clock. It said three o'clock as he knew it would. The past four weeks he'd kept waking up at the same hour. It didn't help that Judith was cold-rife and the duvet was so thick it was like being in a padded envelope.

'Are you okay?' asked Judith.

'Fine,' he said, swinging himself out of bed.

He was still rocked by the loss of the apple saplings. They'd barely been in the ground a week. When he'd reached the orchard that evening, there were clumps of upturned earth like molehills left in their place. He was certain though, he'd told Judith, it wasn't malicious. Thieves were all it was. It was too easy to be paranoid.

Downstairs, he turned on the tap, listening to the water echo round the belly of the sink, while he drank a cup dry. All he and Judith needed was time. Time eased fear. It hadn't helped that their dog, Duke, had died the week before. They'd get a new dog, a real hound that'd put the fear of God into everyone. A Rottweiler even. He laughed to himself, imagining how he'd traverse the fields in a baseball cap with a Rottweiler at his side, like an urban drug dealer. He pulled the dressing gown away from his skin to let some cool air circulate and went back up.

Judith was lying face-up, awake, as he heeled back into bed. He dragged a little of the duvet over him. Now that he was older, he kept overheating. Judith had joked with him how well matched they were — with the furriness on his body and the frizz on her face, they were like two wee bears these days.

He felt her hand on his shoulder.

'Are you stressed?' she asked.

Her fingertips felt rough from all her gardening. He remembered seeing all the little cuts in them and he felt a surge of warmth at how for years she'd kept wounding herself in their garden and had never complained.

'Erwin, it's time we really talked about this,' she said. 'My cousin's doing well with his farm in Northumberland. We could always go there.'

He sighed and turned back onto his sleeping side.

'Let it lie a bit, love,' he said. 'It'll all be grand, you'll see.'

It was Thursday evening and about ten people were sitting silently in the hall, the backs of their chairs pressed against the wall.

As Erwin came down the stairs, he could hear Judith giving off to Martha in the living room.

'Your sandals are on the wrong feet. How many times do I have to tell you, the buckles go on the outside!'

Erwin cringed inwardly at the shenanigans as he passed his patients and said, 'Good evening,' before going through to his study.

He looked at the small phials on the shelf. He'd need to order more of the charcoal and ginger extract. They were running low on the figwort. Judith grew most of the herbs in the garden and dried them in the kitchen. There were even some rare herbs from his mother's time, in spite of the day Martha had mistaken them for weeds and tried to assassinate them with Paraquat. The patients were never charged, though he could have ripped the arm out of it had he chosen; instead, he left an open biscuit tin at the edge of his desk in the old country way, leaving it up to them how much to pay. All the remedies had been passed down by his mother. It suddenly struck him that he'd have to write them down and pass them on to his own son. He'd never thought about it before.

Judith popped her head round the door and saw that he was ready. She ushered in the first patient, a tall girl who bowed her head a little as if in a mark of respect to him, though it was just to avoid the low lintel. Our wee hobbit house, Judith fondly called it. He recognized the girl as the one who'd told him she had cancer.

'Hello, Mr White,' she said, sitting down.

To his patients, he was Mr White rather than Erwin, although he'd never asked for it.

The girl told him that the oncologist had been amazed by how much her tumour had shrunk. 'A miracle,' she'd been told.

'That's very good news,' said Erwin, smiling. 'We'll just keep going as we're going then.'

He'd long since stopped wondering to what extent his herbs really helped and to what extent it was the hope he gave his patients. He gave her the phials of curcumin, tapped a little powder from three jars into a bowl, then divided it out into ten plastic bags. He silently prayed for God to continue to help the girl, as he closed up the bags. When he said goodbye, he could see a little vein in her neck that was bright blue and he knew that the herbs were working well in her blood.

After she left, he felt a peace grow within him. Folk came to see him from all six counties, and from further afield. Catholics came too. Even a Muslim from Lurgan had once come to see him. He had a strong feeling he'd be safe on his land no matter what. Since so many people's lives depended on him, surely God would make sure that no one would hurt him.

The last patient had just left when Robert Girvan arrived.

'How's the pigs?' asked Martha, opening the back door to him.

'Oh, grand, grand,' said Robert and Martha giggled happily. She'd always loved pigs and, with the contrariness of her damaged mind, loved them even more after hearing her father's story of the sow.

Erwin leapt to his feet at Robert's voice. Robert owned the farm five miles away, but rarely visited.

He limped visibly as he made his way into the living room. He was nearing seventy and, in spite of his son taking over the farm, he was a great worker. He'd spruced himself up for his visit but his hair was still crushed down from the woollen hat he wore in the fields. He had a tan line right across his forehead.

'I was sorry to hear about your trees,' he told Erwin after they'd shaken hands.

'I know,' said Erwin. 'Bad craic alright but I put it down to thieves.'

Robert shook his head uncertainly. 'There was a car out watching us last night. I went over to the gate, but it belted off down the road, don't know who it was.'

Judith went out, not wanting to listen.

'And did you see another Irish tricolour's put up on the main road? What about that, Erwin?' Robert looked at him, his eyes ripe like misty blueberries from his cataracts. 'I don't want to sell up. At my age! I just heard Hughie's farm was sold today. Catholic buyer of course.'

'No harm in that.'

'Oh, no harm at all, but they won't be under threat like us.'

Erwin nodded. He thought of the family grave: Abraham White, Isaac and Isabel White, generations of the Whites on this land. Only the other day, he'd passed by the old graveyard and gone in. His father's plot was still covered in the herbs Judith had planted all those years ago.

'I went to see one of their politicians,' continued Robert, 'but not one bit of interest he showed.'

'Was it Gerry Adams?' asked Martha suddenly.

'No, no, not him,' said Robert and Erwin looked at her sharply, newly conscious of the hard click of her needles. He'd almost forgotten she was there, drinking everything in. She was knitting another jacket for the orphans in bright yellow wool. It had taken her a while to understand that she couldn't knit a white jacket as in Eastern Europe they buried babies in white.

'Well, it's not so bad,' said Robert, aware that Martha might be feeling the darkness of their conversation and switching to talk of the low grain prices.

Judith came back in just as Robert was leaving. He had difficulty getting out of his chair.

'I've a sore shin,' he said sheepishly.

'Sinn Fein,' crowed Martha, proud of her cleverness.

'Martha!' admonished Judith and went on quickly, 'It's the wet weather affects it, isn't it?'

'Aye, but it's always wet here, isn't it?' twinkled Robert. 'It's either sun and showers or showers and sun.'

After Robert had gone, Erwin went out to the bins in the yard. It was dark, but little petals of white from the early cherry tree whirled around the gravel. His mood always rose at these playful spirals. When he was young, his mother had told him it was the confetti from the fairy weddings that were held every night in their field. He stood there, wondering if he and Robert should gather all the farmers in the area and start a public outcry.

'What are you doing out there, Daddy?' called Martha from the hall.

'Nothing,' he said, going back inside. 'Nothing at all.'

Judith asked for the umpteenth time that morning, 'What time are you going again?'

'His flight's in at four,' said Erwin, 'So I'll leave at three.'

'What if his plane crashes?' asked Martha, knowing that Judith was in such a good mood she wouldn't get a scold. 'I'm not going to another bloody funeral.'

'I've his steak bought for dinner,' beamed Judith, ignoring her. 'Aye, we're getting there.'

Erwin laughed. 'We're getting there,' was one of Judith's favourite phrases.

'Half the countryside's been phoning up to ask when he's coming,' said Judith. 'Apparently he said he was on his way on that Facebook and they've all got wind of it.'

'They'd be round at a fart's turn, them lot,' chipped in Martha, cheerily.

The boy's coming home, said Erwin to himself delightedly, as he loaded bags of potassium onto the tractor. He'd already decided something, though he hadn't told Judith. He'd let James rest a day after his journey, then suggest a trip over to Northumberland to see Judith's cousin's farm. If they were going to leave this part of the world, now would be the right time before James got settled back into the way of things again. The image of Hughie Glass, shot sitting on his tractor in the middle of his field, hadn't been so frightening when he thought only of himself. He was fifty-five, he was old enough to die, but as for his son... The past two nights, he hadn't slept for thinking of it.

He shrugged off his dark thoughts, started up the tractor and headed out to the orchard. The morning was foggy but the sun would burn it off later, though for now it hung low in the sky, a big ethereal red ball that you could look at full in the face. He felt cosy in the fog, protected by its thickness. As he drove past the hawthorns, he could smell the ditch of wild garlic and he stopped the tractor and jumped off, ripping out a clump that he put in his coat pocket. Judith loved to cook with it.

Nearing the orchard, he could see the boughs of the apple trees as curved as Celtic runes against the parchment of fog. He imagined what it would be like in a different land with long, rolling wheat fields and bigger skies. The farm belonging to Judith's cousin was called Windgate Moor and the wintriness of its name made him shiver. Who knew, maybe he would love it when he got there and having family around would make it home. As far as he knew, his ancestors had originally come from the Scottish borders, so it would be almost like returning home. Sure, maybe James had made contacts in Australia and they could buy a farm there, he laughed to himself. He loved the bones of that boy, so much so his own bones ached. It was only right that James would decide where the next generation of Whites would live.

He lifted the first bag off the back of the tractor. After all that rain the land was leached — aye, the trees needed their powders and potions just like people needed them. It was his job to minister to everyone. His father had planted some of these trees when he was eighty, knowing he'd never see the fruit of them, but they were still going strong. Erwin slapped one of the trunks, and he could almost feel the warmth of life in it.

He turned, hearing the crack of twigs underfoot.

He couldn't see anyone, but he could tell from the weight of the sound it was human. My Christ, he said to himself. He wanted to run but he wasn't near the road.

Two dark figures were coming out of the fog towards him. Two men. His heart was beating wildly but strangely his mind felt tame.

His father's words—'Always stand your ground!'—resonated in his head. They came to a halt about fifty yards away. He stared at them, trying to imprint them on his memory, because he instinctively knew that if he survived, it would be important. One man was young, the other older, like a father and son it seemed to him.

After a few seconds, it occurred to him that they might only be there to intimidate. He slowly turned his back to them and walked towards his tractor. He felt his boots sink into the muddy ground and he could hardly lift his feet; it was as if the land had already decided he belonged there and its softness was opening up and pulling him in. The smell of wet, rotting roots flooded his nostrils. 'Please God,' he kept praying with each step, the panic growing in him.

He got into his tractor and started it. He didn't dare to look back at the men. He set off, moving quickly up through the gears. An image suddenly came into his head of the sow from his nightmares, wearing a baby's white jacket, scurrying for its life through his garden, digging up through the herbs, trying to hide beneath them. Its big coarse snout grunting and squealing. Its terrified features melting away to be replaced by the big, glowing sun, which was now scorching a hole through the white skin of the fog.

He didn't stop to close the gate to the orchard but went on. Seconds passed and he began to breathe more easily. He still hoped he would see his son later. From his seat, in the distance he could see Judith bent over, tending to the herbs, her cardiganed back like a grey boulder fixed in the landscape. The hotting sun was baking a new smell in the grass; one that had the sweetness of apples.

SONG FOR A POLISH STRANGER

'Love songs shouldn't be about love,' said Fergal of the song being piped through the radio. 'They should be about real things like women picking up their men's underwear.'

Claire cringed for him as the Disability Processing Section went quiet — even the music seemed to fall silent in deference — and all eyes turned to the supervisor, Donna.

'Fergal, have you read your EO1247?' Donna asked, knowing that he had not. She ploughed on in her harsh country voice like a County Down tractor. 'Well, you should have. It's about equal opportunity.'

'Sorry,' mumbled Fergal pinkly. Claire fired him a sympathetic look because he was the one source of fun in the office, even if or probably due to the fact he was non-PC. Not that she fancied him. Like most of the men in the predominantly female office he was a little tubbified, perhaps even oestrogenised from the atmosphere, but at least his mind still flexed.

For the rest of the Friday afternoon the office worked on mutely, everyone floating off on the love songs, unconsciously moving to the beat on their swivel chairs, even the copying machines clicking into the radio rhythm. The fifth floor looked out over a backdrop of city roofs and Claire could see her reflection in the window like a fragile hologram suspended against the skyscape. She seemed paler than ever. The nights out followed by the long days in the office were taking their toll.

At four o'clock when everyone was packing up, Fergal sidled up to Claire.

'So, are you off out for some pints tonight?'

'Should be,' she grinned.

He was always asking about her social life. She couldn't decide if he derived a vicarious thrill from her adventures or was trying to show her up in front of Donna.

'You better watch it,' he warned with a hint of a flirt in his smile. 'I was just reading that women who drink get more sexually aggressive.'

Fergal's jaw dropped as he realized he'd made his second blunder of the day. All eyes turned to Donna who shook her head in disapproval.

'Come out tonight then and we'll put your theory to the test,' Claire challenged him.

Fergal blushed and lowered his head, pretending to tidy his desk.

Claire almost leapt through the office doors. It was a relief to get away from the sterile off-white walls and cooped-up energies. The first thing she always did was look to the hills. Today in the April sun they were like soft wheaten bread, covered in a floury haze risen up from the warm dustbowl of Belfast. As she headed home, starlings with golden tipped wings swooped up from under the Albert Bridge.

She wasn't sure what she would do that night. She thought of Owen. She'd met him in the pub the week before and they'd swapped numbers. Owen was ten years younger than her, with black hair and skin the shade of Guinness foam, but she knew all it would lead to was sex. Microwave sex she termed it: sex that was hot, quick and filling at the time but was ultimately full of salt tears, empty and bad for your health.

She turned onto the Cregagh Road where the red-brick terraces hirpled down the hill. The new greenery on the trees was soft and lettuce-fresh. Some leaves were still concertinaed in their buds, about to fan forth into the light — she always found herself jealous of nature and how it could renew itself. She was thirty-five herself now. Oh, sure, she looked young for her age, but still. She'd recently been for a smear test and when she'd asked how she was 'down there', the nurse had answered, 'to the left and a bit prolapsed.' Of course, it had been a bit much to hope to be told she had a very youthful example of a vagina and cervix, but a few positive words would have been reassuring.

At Willowfield Church she noticed they had erected a giant wooden cross for Easter. Draped over the cross was an empty white robe, and it seemed that Jesus had done a Houdini. Like most men, she mused. A couple of women were standing outside, serving hot cross buns, and Claire had just taken one when a man in white overalls stepped out in front of her carrying a split-open pig, its pink legs bouncing off his shoulders in a slightly obscene way. She couldn't take her eyes off the carcase till the man veered away into the butcher's.

The sun was strong on the sheltered side of the street. Some red jellied sweets had melted on the pavement like bits of a molten heart. Nearby, candy Love Hearts, crushed by passing footsteps, seemed to be chalking out letters on the pavement. She followed the sticky sweet trail onto My Lady's Road where children were spiralling themselves crazy and staggering, as if in imitation of the drunks who tottered out of The Longfellow. She stood a while and watched their antics. One child had tied a rope round a lamp post and was hurling herself round on it. A little boy was sitting on the kerb playing a battered red, white and blue drum with a couple of pens as makeshift sticks. Claire was so absorbed in the scene, it took her a while to tune in to some deep neighbouring chuckles. When she glanced across, she noticed that a man was standing beside her. He was blond, of a bigger build than most of the East Belfast locals and wore a different expression, less worried and more confident. He was dressed in a long-sleeved t-shirt but his left arm only filled the top, then the sleeve tapered away and was tucked into the side of his jeans. She'd seen him around the streets several times before, their eyes meeting as they'd passed each other. On both occasions, she'd wondered about his arm but these days you were supposed to be blind to disabilities.

'Those kids are funny, yeah?' he said, amused.

'Crazy.'

'Must be spring madness.'

She guessed from his accent he was Eastern European.

'You're not from round here, are you?'

'I am. I live that way,' he said, pointing, just to tease her. 'No, I know what you mean. I'm from Poland.'

Images of red clay roads, poppies blowing kisses from wheat fields, the old town centres and the pubs, especially the pubs, spun in her mind.

'Oh, Poland. I used to teach English there. I loved it—the lakes in Mazury, Poronin, the salt mines at Wieliczka...'

She'd been there ten years ago and it still gave her a pang.

It surprised him. 'You know more in Poland than me! I'm from a village outside Radom. I've only been here two months—that's why my English is so bad.'

'Come on, it's better than some of the locals'.'

'I know. Two months and I still can't understand them. *How's about ye?*' he imitated in a harsh Ulster accent that made Claire laugh out loud. 'What are you all saying? What?'

They began to walk down the road together.

'So what do you make of Belfast?'

'Weather is terrible,' he smiled. 'And the beer.'

'Zywiec, Lech, Tyskie,' she recited. 'God, one year in Krakow and the only words I learnt were the beers.'

'Good student!'

'So, what brought you to Belfast?' she asked.

'A job in computers. Very boring.'

'Yeah?'

'Yeah, I'm like some type of cyber security guard. It's mad. I help to protect all the millions that companies make — but me, where's my millions?'

'It can't be worse than mine. I process forms for the disabled. All they do is complain...' She stopped short, as it dawned on her that he could be one of her clients. 'Not that the disabled don't have reason to complain,' she hastily added, ashamed.

'Oh, it's fine. I like that you are honest.'

She started to tell him about Donna and Fergal. It felt so inconsequential she wasn't even sure if he followed most of it, but it didn't seem to matter. The moment came when they neared the turn-off to her own street and she should have said goodbye to him. But as they passed a line of cherry trees, a gust of wind blizzarded the white petals over their heads and Claire nearly shouted out with the joy of it. They exchanged a shy, happy smile as they scuffed through the petal-drifts on the pavement. Up ahead were a few of the boarded-up windows daubed with 'Locals Only'. Some Polish families had been forced out in the past few weeks, and Claire immediately felt the shame of it, though she said nothing.

'I would have stayed in Poland, but I had to leave,' he explained, sensing her embarrassment. 'Even the big cities have no jobs and it's more difficult with this...' He raised his left shoulder, to illustrate the emptiness of his sleeve.

'I know. It must be hard for you.'

'There you are. A disabled man complaining again!' he joked.

They walked on together through streets Claire didn't recognise. 'Following a stranger,' she thought as her heart began to speed; she didn't know how it would end.

'I live here,' he finally said, slowing down.

The glass panel in the front door was covered in chipboard.

'What happened?' she asked.

'Someone must have smashed it.'

'Oh, God. Because you're Polish?'

'Probably. I wasn't at home,' he said, shrugging it off. 'No big deal.'

He turned towards her and she could see the contours of his body through his t-shirt. His hollow sleeve quivered in the breeze.

'You want coffee?' he asked.

She hesitated. She knew what he wanted from the look in his eyes.

'But I don't even know you.'

'Come on. Do I look dangerous?'

He reached out gently to touch her hair. She looked at him, confused, then he showed her the little heart-shaped petal between his fingers before the wind ushered it away.

'So what's your name?'

'Claire.'

'I'm Tomasz.'

'I'll come in for a while,' she heard herself say.

He opened the door. She was barely in when his mouth swooped to hers, the sheer speed of his move rocking her back against the wall. For a second, it felt as ludicrous as a scene out of a movie, making her wonder if he was genuine, but the kiss was so warm and deep, she fell into it, kissing him back. He closed the door over with his foot and the hall went darker. She pulled away from him, wary of entering a strange place.

'You live alone?' she checked.

'No. With two guys from Radom but they're at work.' He inclined his head towards the stairs and held out his hand. 'Do you want to..?'

She hesitated again, glancing down. His open palm looked strong. A suffocating image of the office flashed into her mind and she imagined herself going wild, upturning the desks, flinging the forms into the air. She felt her skin slide into his.

The blinds in his bedroom blew outwards in a bluster of wind, making chinging sounds against the glass as if in welcome. The bed-clothes were a midnight blue. The room was so tidy it was like he'd expected her. He closed the blinds from prying eyes. With jittery fingers they undressed each other in the dusk of the room. She unbuckled his belt and lifted his t-shirt up from his waist. She paused a second, scared suddenly — what if his mangled arm repulsed her? All those words she entered into the database each day: shaking flesh, night sweats, weeping sores, prosthetic limbs, pain...

She peeled his t-shirt from his body. She couldn't help staring. The bulk of his shoulder bulged into bicep, then narrowed for an inch into nothingness. His stump wasn't what she'd expected — it was muscled but unscarred, unblemished as if it had been formed that way.

He cast her a rueful smile.

'A car crash. When I was sixteen. Yes,' he mused, remembering. 'It made me grow up very quick.'

'It must have been so hard.'

'My friend who drove. He died.' He glanced down self-consciously. 'Every time I look at myself, I think of him.'

'I'm sorry.'

'No, I'm lucky to be alive.'

It felt smooth as driftwood to her touch.

'I think it's beautiful,' she told him.

His whole body felt planed to perfection, grained with light blond. He seemed to shine in the shaded room.

'It's been so long for me,' she confessed to him, lying down on the bed.

'How long?'

'Eight months since I had anyone.'

'That's a long time,' he whispered, cupping her chin, drawing her face towards his. 'Take whatever you need.'

Their fingers rippled over each other's skin. She could hear her own blood-beat pulsing within her head. His lips buzzed around her blindly, to her mouth, her throat, her chest, going lower and lower. He was pushing her body into different angles, becoming more pressing, insistent. The backs of her thighs jagged in pain, making her call out to him. 'Slowly,' she breathed and, little by little, her sinews began to yield and melt. His hand was so broad it felt like two, wrapping itself round her waist, easing her into the rhythm of his hips. Soon she began to feel his flesh beating inside her, even stronger than her own heart.

Afterwards, they lay together, the vestiges of his arm enfolding her like it was a gull's wing and she felt safe there. She noticed the same far-away, blank look on his face as when he'd been inside her body, sex-dazed. It was as though he was afraid that words could break the fragile wonder of the past hour, the quiet beauty they'd just shared. The breeze pattered on the blinds. Then the harsh beep of a text broke through the softness.

'Sorry,' she said and he laughed.

'I have to go now anyway,' he said, getting up. 'To my friend's house. He's meeting his landlord. He needs me to translate for him.'

She got up too, her legs weak and achey, feeling faint. She felt herself move around like a shaky foal who had just come out the womb. When she lifted up her jeans, coins flew out of her pocket, clattering onto the bare floorboards.

'My God, it's like I'm paying you!' she joked as he helped pick them up.

'What? I'm only worth ninety p?'

They pulled on the rest of their clothes in silence. For the first time, she was aware that his alarm clock was ticking loudly.

Doubts began to flutter through her. What if he was one of those guys who came to a new country and was only after conquests? It crossed her mind how he had been the first to speak, how easily he had picked her up. Maybe he even used his disability as a lure with which to fascinate women and rouse their sympathy. When she'd admitted how long it had been since she'd slept with someone, he hadn't reciprocated. For all she knew, he could have been with scores of women since he'd arrived.

'Hey, but what about that coffee?' she asked, pretending to be let down.

'Next time.'

He was smiling as he wrote down his number. He tucked it into her pocket, down the back of her jeans, drawing her to him. A wave of warmth flowed over her. She felt foolish for having doubted him.

Her hand slipped into his again as she let him lead her down the stairs. For a second time she noticed the darkness cast by the boarded door. It made her shiver.

'Aren't you going to move somewhere safe?' she said.

'No. I'd rather fight. You don't understand. When you lose part of your body you're a survivor, you can't be beaten.'

'But why did you choose Belfast? It's a difficult city.'

'A friend came. He said the people are great. Well, except the ones with the bricks.'

'True.'

'Look, I want to see you again,' he said, opening the door to a rush of light.

'I want to see you too.'

'Then call me.'

'We can always go out for some terrible Irish beer,' she grinned, kissing him goodbye.

It was so bright in the sun outside, she had to screw up her eyes. The wind had strengthened, making her feel cold after the warmth of Tomasz's room. A small tear came to her left eye and she wiped it away.

She finally looked at her text. It was from Owen, wanting to see her that night. She quickly deleted it.

Claire walked home, the words, 'next time, next time, next time' refraining in her head. The trees she passed looked more muscular than before. The barks were rough and pollarded, she could hear the branches rocking with an energy unlike the rhythm of everyday life. Above them, it was turning to evening and the orange brightness of the sky was pearling like the soft colour of the light bulbs flicking on in the windows. Something was still beating inside her. She couldn't stop thinking of Tomasz's smooth limb, the sheer strength and vitality of it. Under the opalescent skies, a love song they kept playing on the radio at work filtered back to her. She watched as one of the drunks headed home from The Longfellow, leaning forward against the wind, only to stagger forward when it dropped. A small band of kids, voices splintered, skeltered past her, as they ran out once more to play. She reached into her pocket for the scrap of paper Tomasz had given her, curled it round her fingers and held it tight.

LOVE HISTORY

I'd come home from abroad and was staying at my parents' house in Berwick for the first time in three years and hopefully the last time for another three. Just to give you an illustration, my mother put a throw over the cream armchair of the new, oversized meringue suite, so I wouldn't mark it. I suggested she put a glass case over it and have a tour of paying visitors—which went down like a lead zeppelin of course. Over the years she'd become obsessive about cleanliness and regarded me as some scruffy, boisterous dog returning home from kennels.

The day after I got back, I saw James. He was standing in the street chatting to one of his friends so I went over to say hello.

'Emma, I haven't seen you in years!' He was smiling, which was unusual, as he generally scorned such excesses as smiling and dancing, being more of a cool guy.

It had been about five years and had he changed. He'd put on a few stone and his face had broadened into fleshiness. Before he'd been fairly pale but now he had a florid tone. I had to admit he still looked good. Just different, a physical type that once would have been called sanguine—the earthy look of a man who indulged himself. He still had the green eyes, and cheekbones like his were strong enough to carry any amount of weight.

He'd been fishing that morning, pulling in the lobster crieves, so he was in his work clothes. I liked that. It gave him an air of Lady Chastity's lover. And I liked hunters. I understood them because I was one myself. We all wore our scars invisibly but could sense them in each other. Hunting within the boundaries of society was known as pulling.

We chatted. James's life hadn't changed any. Neither had mine, it had just relocated. Without preamble, he started telling me about the women in his life.

'This one I'm seeing I met on the bus when I went to visit a friend in prison. Her husband, a right gangland thug, was in for murdering a lover of hers. I did think about it but... Anyway, the first nights I stayed over she made me sleep in her spare room and I was getting sick of it. Then one night she came into my room, and after that there was no peace for me. She was hotter than hell.'

I was happy to see him. He had a romantic soul coupled with a love of sluttish women. I didn't have his fisherman's patience. It was more a case of what I saw I had to have. I was pretty sure I was born to live, die, eat, sleep and have sex. I couldn't preserve my appetite for late night meals. I slept when I wanted, I'd die when I was ready. And sex was no different.

The vibes shook me. As he walked away, I reacquainted myself with the beautiful sight of his firm behind leading up to a straight, broad back. And his sexuality came from somewhere deeper. You saw it in his walk—his steps were cagey, his fists were closed and his head was held low, watchful like an animal. As I say, I love hunters.

We arranged to meet on Saturday. It was funny but the thought of seeing him again made me nervous. Like when I was a child and used to love the idea of fairground rides—that was until the moment of getting on and the butterflies would start. I was alright once it was up and going but it was that moment just before...

We met on a Saturday night in a seamy pub. On the downside, the neon lighting showed up the dandruff on dark clothes but on the up-side, it made your teeth look white. Well, you couldn't have it all.

James looked good in his long leather coat. He wore a dress shirt trimmed with lace, which added a touch of flair to the hard man look. The top button of the shirt strained sexily across his chest.

'You look good,' I said.

'Yes?' He seemed shy that I'd said it. 'But don't mention the shoes. Everyone's already taken the rise out of them.'

They were stylish. I couldn't see anything wrong with them. Though I probably wouldn't know. My clothes never go out of style for the simple reason that they were never in style in the first place.

'Thanks for your vote of confidence, Mrs Sensible Shoes,' smiled James.

'They're the only sensible part of me.'

'I know. You're stark mad otherwise. Look, there's Karen Coulter. She tried to get me to ride her last year but I wouldn't. She got her breasts out in the street to show me and her daughter started screaming, "Mum, you dirty old slut!" There was hell on.'

He told me more stories. He didn't talk much about Vivienne, the woman he'd been living with since I'd first met him. He didn't ask me anything. Like a lot of men, he prefers to get his information about a woman's view from a book like *Forum Sex Letters*, because it's more impersonal. Though he cracks on that women love sex as much as men, he is imbued with a supreme belief that man is an adventurer and woman is merely an adventuree.

He broke off in mid-flow. 'Can I ask you something, Emma? What do you think of me?'

I slid my hand into his coat and pinched his side. 'Gorgeous.'

'No, really.'

'Is this a crisis of confidence?'

'Hardly. It's just after five years of not seeing you...'

'Okay. I see you as intelligent and as someone who loves adventure.'

He was pleased. 'You're right.'

I should have stopped there but I never could one hundred per cent flatter. Men hated that about me, it was a sackable offence with most of them but I still couldn't bring myself to push the right buttons. 'You also have no self-control.'

'True. Neither do you.'

James and I sat down at a table with some of the old gang. I spoke to Lisa, who I hadn't seen in years. She was now married with three children.

'I didn't know you were with James,' she said.

'Well, we've seen each other on and off over the years.'

'Are you both thinking about getting married?'

'No.'

'But one day you may fall in love with him without realising. That's how it happens.' She was pretty and a genuinely good person but a bit simplistic. 'Don't you love him?'

Some people just came from a different religion. There was no doubt I felt an emotion halfway between fondness and lust for James but lacking the eternal aspect.

'I love men,' I said. 'Anyway, he has a couple of women on the go,' I added because I knew she'd understand that better even though I'd have to put up with her feeling sympathy for me.

James had just finished speaking to some guy. 'Sad bastard,' he said, shaking his head. 'He's never had a woman. The only reason he's tolerated at this table is because he'll be buying the women a drink.'

I turned to look. The guy was predictably weak-looking.

'Can you not keep your eyes off him?' joked James. 'I think you fancy him.'

'Well, there's not much competition here.'

'Thank you.'

I put my hand on his knee and he put his hand between my legs. It was dark and we were close together so we weren't being overly obvious. I looked down. He never wore underwear, considering it too feminine, and I could see the bulge of his cock in his jeans quite clearly. It turned me on and I had to stop myself from touching.

'Another drink?' I offered.

'I'll get it. You unemployed people, you're a drain on society, so I'll pay.'

'You talk like my father.'

'Yes, but I'm better at sex than your father.'

'My mother seems happy,' I said. I imagined my parents at it on the cream sofa and it didn't bear thinking about.

'Well, I could re-educate her. She might consider me, now I've gone all grey.'

'You're not grey.'

He passed his hand over his short black hair to show me the flecks of silver. In the lighting it appeared black. The years didn't seem to have changed him much at all. I couldn't stop looking at him. It was like being able to revisit a favourite painting in a gallery of lovers.

'Look at the token sexy chick in here,' he said, pointing at a woman dancing. 'Why is it women are always nicer than men? Look at the men round here. They're beasts.'

'Not all of them. Women have bland bodies for my taste. Men are better — saltier and harder.'

James frowned. I had said the wrong thing. It was strange. He had a jealousy of all men and he loved women to agree that women were the more beautiful of the species. It was just his line.

'Go on then. Who have you slept with out of all the men here?'

'That's a thorny question. Or should I say horny?'

'Just answer it.'

'Him.'

There were a few faces and bodies I recognized, but instead I pointed out a guy I'd never met before. I'd glanced over at him a couple of times already, because he kept pulling his trousers up by the waistband, a habit drawing attention to his slim hips which I already thirsted for.

'Him! I'm surprised. He's got a giant nose.'

'Well, you know what they say about men with big noses...'

'Well, fuck off to him then.'

'And you fuck off to your sexy chick!' I shouted back at him as he walked away.

I went up to the guy. He was standing at the bar and turned his head towards me as I came up beside him.

'Have I met you before, at a party or somewhere?' he asked.

'No, but maybe you've seen me on TV.'

'I don't watch TV.'

'I don't go to parties.'

I liked him. When he smiled, his eyes went like inkblots in crumpled paper. He had a gap between his front teeth and I longed to dart my tongue through it. And, of course, he had a strong nose. I called it strong, not big, and that was the difference between James's gender and mine. He was broad-chested under a tight white t-shirt and his hair was shaved high up his neck, revealing folds of sinew that I wanted instantly to grab with my fingers and bite. Tattoos were curling under his short sleeves like snakes coiling out from under cover. As for those slim hips encased in black trousers with white pockets that were splitting at the seams, stretched to their limits.

'I'm not drinking any more of this beer,' he said. 'It's terrible.'

'What else is there to do on a Saturday night but drink beer?'

'Do you have to ask?'

'I live with my parents.'

'Aw, diddums,' he laughed. 'I don't.'

I was excited. I had a last guzzle of my beer, then left the dregs.

As we left, I checked behind me. James was in deep conversation with some guys he knew. He looked drunk, even a bit degenerate and ageing. His colour was impossibly high. I would let him expend his worst efforts on someone else tonight.

His name was Liam. He had intense eyes, so intense that they got through to you from the farthest distance. He had a flat a couple of streets away. It was a nice place, fairly modern, blue furnished. He was a builder. I don't know what it was but I loved workmen. I've always had fantasies about having my own home and getting plumbers, chippies, gasmen to call. But especially window cleaners. It was almost worth the hassle of getting a mortgage for that alone.

He had a CD player in his bedroom and he switched it on loud. People who liked to have sex to music were either very good or very tragic. We lay on the bed and kissed, fully clothed. I felt that broad neck writhing under my lips and we began to pull each other's tops off.

'Wait,' he said and reached into the bedside drawer. He took out a condom and then rolled his trousers off. He was incredibly muscular, right down to his toned, wired toes.

He went out to the bathroom. I took the opportunity of throwing the condom still in its wrapper out the window.

'Where is it?' he asked when he came back in.

'Out the window.'

'You're drunk.'

He took another one out. There was a photo of him on the bedside table, on a bicycle with a crash helmet.

'That's you?' I said.

'Yes. I ski too. I like sports, do you?'

'The only dangerous sport I do is sex without a condom.'

'You're mad.'

He softly kissed the base of my neck and I quivered at the warm breath and coolness of his tongue. He kissed me on the lips, then slowly worked his way down my body. It was a tantalizing slowness that made me shift and move with almost a desperation to be gratified further. I felt the tip of his cock on my leg and it was already wet. He slid down the bed and gave me the steady head-dart till he had me tingling. He immediately entered. He was on top of me and it suited me that way because I could hold on to his rocks of buttocks while he dug and stabbed inside. They were pure muscled like an athlete's and I could feel the individual strain of each strand of sinew and it excited me because it was life and power. I felt the wild rock of his hips and a dizziness in my ears like I was high in a tree during a storm. He came with a moan and I kept him inside, squeezing him now and then while he gave little sighs in response.

When I got up and put my clothes on in the morning, Liam asked, 'Do you have a boyfriend?'

'Sometimes.'

'What do you mean, sometimes? Either you do or you don't.'

'Do you really want to know if I have a boyfriend or are you asking if you can see me again?'

'Both.'

'Sure, honey, give me your number.'

'You won't give me yours? Is that why you're rushing off?'

'Look, Liam.' My head was griping. It was trying to inveigle my stomach into feeling the same way. 'Have you got any spirits in the flat?'

'I never drink in the flat. It's my policy.'

'Then give me a kiss to make me feel better.'

I told him he was fantastic and that raised a grin from him. Maybe he'd expected too much from me. A fatal mistake. Sure I liked him enough but I never wanted to be pinned down by anyone – except in bed of course.

I got home at eleven thirty.

'Have a nice night, darling?' my Mum asked. 'Where were you?'

'Took a carry-out back to Michelle's and crashed there.'

'You up to your old tricks again?' asked my Dad.

'Yes. You should see my trick with a ping pong ball, Dad.'

I'd just had a shower when James phoned.

'Good night last night?'

'Fine.'

'Can you be round at three today?'

'If you're free.'

'Vivienne starts work at three,' he explained and I could almost hear the smile, the lips lifting over the teeth. 'Make sure you're wearing the smallest pair of panties.'

'Right. I'll just pop out to Lilliput and I'll be over at three.'

'You're not going out, are you?' asked my father. 'Alan's up here on business and he's coming to lunch today.'

Alan was my cousin. He had a regular job and a regular girlfriend, which sounded all a bit irregular to me. He had no fun but he did have a pension. As my Dad reminded and reminded me. I asked Dad how he thought I would cope with running a pension? Besides, I had no interest in starting up a bed and breakfast on the continent.

My father detested my flippancy and he probably had a point. I was in my immature early thirties and couldn't help it.

'So, Emma, what's your plan now you're home?' cousin Alan asked me breezily at the dining table.

'I don't have plans.'

'Right. You go with the flow.'

'What flow?'

'You're pretty relaxed about life, aren't you? I have a sneaking admiration for you, even though I could never be like that myself. I always have to know what I'm doing in the next two or three years.'

'You should be careful. The longer you map out the future, the madder you are. Remember Stalin with his five-year plan?'

After lunch was over, I went round to James's house.

When he answered the door, his trousers were already unbuttoned and unzipped. What a guy. He was always hot for it.

We went up to the bedroom. It had changed in the five years. There were frilly-edged curtains and lamps.

'Vivienne's home improvements,' said James. He took his trousers off and got into bed. I sneaked enough of a peak to establish that he wasn't fat-stomached, just bigger built. He looked good. I thought his legs had been too skinny before. I hoped that I hadn't got worse with the years, though I was sure I hadn't. And, even if I had, I didn't honestly care.

'You're a real home pigeon now,' I teased.

'You know, she got me when I was drunk and asked if she could have a fruit blender and I handed the money over. I'd never have given it to her sober. A fruit blender! It takes about twelve apples to make one tiny glass of juice! And you have to chop the apples up yourself!'

He was on one of his flights of outrage as of old.

'Are you getting all Dylan Thomasy on me, James?'

'Yes. Rage, rage against the dying of the fruit blender. And it will die because I'm going to smash it against the wall soon enough.'

I'd taken off my clothes slowly, so he could get a look at my sexy underwear ensemble. He looked with sly eyes. Then I joined him in bed.

'What happened last night with you and big nose?' he asked, putting his arm around my shoulders.

I was surprised. He'd never asked me things like that before. Because of the sheer novelty of the question I lied. 'I couldn't have ever slept with anyone with such a big nose.'

'Bet you did.'

'Okay, I did. And he had a great body. But he was no good in bed. He was a Pyramus.'

'A what?'

'A Pyramus. A tragic lover. You know, tragic as in bad. Shakespeare's *Pyramus and Thisbe*.'

'Don't talk Shakespeare to me.'

He didn't get it, or didn't want to, but he wasn't bothered because I'd confirmed for him that Liam was useless. And it was in my interest for James to think that, as it would inspire him to give a surpassing performance to show me how sex was meant to be. Get into men's minds and men get into your body.

His hand worked its way under my pants.

'What about you last night?' I asked.

'I had sex with an eighteen-year-old over a bench.'

'Really?'

'Yes, and you won't believe what else happened last night. That woman I've been seeing...'

'The murderer's moll.'

'That's right. She phoned up Vivienne, blitzed with drink, and offered to sleep with her.' A big grin spread over his face. 'Vivienne was raging.'

'I bet she was.'

We kissed and our breaths grew deeper as he kneaded me. I held his cock in my hand and started to slowly jerk him off. His hardness hit against my leg. I held it tightly, feeling its blood-pumping life between my fingers, then I moved my head down, so I could suck. He moved my legs up past his head to make a sixty-nine. We both licked and sucked like two frenzied bees, and in the force of coming again and again in perpetual orgasm, I took my mouth away to sigh and moan and I just clung on to his cock for life, smothering it and his balls with my lips and face, as my whole body shivered. I felt my clit pulsating, growing bigger and bigger, and bursting with pleasure from the tiniest pain in the core.

Finally I rolled off him, panting, and he exhaled loudly, his eyes gleaming.

I jumped on top and put it in. I sat upright while he stroked away, but as soon as he speeded up, I fell down onto his chest and began to gently bite his shoulder, my face wedged in the darkness, feeling my bone thrusting fast against him, his pubic hair teasing my clitoris.

I dismounted and he turned me onto one side, so that his chest was facing my back and we were both curled up on our sides. He entered my cunt from behind and glided it slowly and gently, interspersing the stroke with stronger jabs, and for some seconds he lay still while I eased him in and out, feeling every inch of his cock inside me. He held on to my shoulders and massaged them softly until finally I felt a tightening grip and, with two or three thrusts, he moaned three times and came.

I looked around at him. His fingers were rubbing his eyes. The skin was inflamed bright red on his neck which was goose-bumped like turkey skin. His face was a fairly vivid pink too. I could feel his heart pounding in his chest. High blood pressure levels. He coughed suddenly. It hit me that he couldn't keep on like this. He drank too much, he ranted too much, he had too much sex, did too much heavy work in the early mornings...

I thanked God I wasn't a man. The truth is women have the strength to rage against it all for longer than men.

I snuggled up to him. I felt I loved him at that moment, vaguely guilty that he had given me more pleasure than he'd got, but that was the way he wanted it. He was one of the greatest sexual givers – to those worth giving to, otherwise you got it over a bench. I was a giver too. I remembered that years back he'd taken umbrage at how I'd got on top and tried to fuck him hard myself. 'It's not a competition, you know, Emma,' he'd said simply.

And I thought how good sex had been with Liam but how greater it was with the deep-stained sentiment of history which lay between me and James.

'Know something?' I said, out of the blue. 'You and me, we're better than heroin.'

'What?'

'It just struck me. People say heroin is a bigger rush, a higher high than sex. Well, they just haven't had sex with us, or else they wouldn't say it.'

He laughed. 'Right. Better than heroin.'

He traced his fingers over my body as we lay there. His touch felt beautiful. It always had. His breath was lulling like the sea.

'I have to get up and record a programme for Vivienne in a moment.'

'Okay.'

'Did I tell you? I'm finally learning to drive.'

'That's great.'

'Yes. Once I've passed my test, I'll be off every Friday, Saturday, going to those addresses in the contact magazines. You know, you can get every kind of sex you want, every combination, every nationality you want.'

'You know, James, next time I go abroad, I want you to come with me...' And I told him about the men and the men and the men...the proud Greek, the intense Japanese, the smouldering Pole, the lunatic Russian, the erotic but neurotic Frenchman...

'You take me, then, Emma,' he said, holding me tightly. 'We'll have a wonderful time with all that sex—we'll have a different one every night. We'll never tire of it and then, when we're old and done, they'll have to ship us home in a crate.'

I already knew that he would never come with me, that he belonged to this town as sure as I belonged to nowhere, but for a moment the shared fantasy of going abroad together gave our love a tender edge before we got lost in each other again.

ODYSSEY

Alex rubbed her knuckles underneath her eyes to wipe away the tears. It was her job to prepare the Greek salad and the onion was very strong. The kitchen was filled with the sizzle from the oven, a joyful sound like cicada song. The lights were on and the window looked out onto a narrow, dusky strip of driveway and field, topped by glowing clouds.

Vangelis came up behind her and hugged her round the waist.

'When you cry, it makes the eyes more beautiful.'

'I like to stand here,' she smiled, 'so that everyone can look in and say, "See how unhappy she is, the poor girl, living with that Greek."'

He growled in his throat at her. 'Yes, I am a bad man but doesn't my cooking smell good?' Vangelis beat his chest like an ape. It made her laugh at him loudly, even exaggeratedly, loving to see him so exuberant because it was the good times. You had to make the most of them.

She took the salad next door where the table was set. In this one large room, there was a dining area and a living space which led into a bedroom alcove. The ground floor was the cheapest to rent in the building. Vangelis, with two children to support since his divorce, couldn't afford any better. A dartboard he had bought for Alex hung on the wall. He'd endured a lot of teasing from his friends for turning his apartment into a British pub.

Through the open door she watched him taste the oil-steeped *fassolatha*. Puckering his lips happily, he murmured praise. He was wearing a tight white t-shirt that showed off his skin as dark as halva, contrasting with the whiteness of his teeth. Strange that she'd come all the way to France only to find herself with a man from Crete.

Car headlights were rolling slowly down the drive. '*Opa, opa!*' Costas shouted above the blare of *bouzouki* music.

They rushed out of their apartment to usher in both their guests, their voices growing giant in the large, cavernous hallway. Alex received kisses on the cheek like red seals of approval.

Immediately, Costas and Iannis headed into the kitchen. Costas took off his jacket, the fragrance of summer air and tobacco escaping from its tucks and folds, and handed Vangelis a jar of black olives. 'From my village,' he explained. '*Speciale.*'

Vangelis set it aside. In the eight months that Alex had lived with Vangelis, she had never known him to thank anyone for a gift. As if he wanted to be the sole provider, the ultimate host, wary of every little hint of gratitude.

Costas inhaled his cigarette with a deep pleasure, stretching his back and rolling his neck. He was about fifty, grey-haired, with eyes well versed in the appraisal of women. His stomach sat tightly in its thin skin of yellow shirt, almost a splendid joke to be proud of, like a water bomb in a condom, mirrored in the little fatty pouches that swelled humorously at the corner of his lips. His whole body was bubbling with a fleshy joy for life.

'How's business, Costa?' Vangelis asked.

Costas, as he liked to remind everyone, was the number one icon seller in France, icons he imported from Greece. His ambition was to build himself a little Parthenon in France, though Alex was never quite sure if this was serious or not.

'Oh, excellent. Today I sold a giant statue of Dionysius to a very powerful man in government. I told him, "Dionysius fucked a lot of goddesses and he looked exactly like you."' Costas tapped the side of his head, opening his eyes wide to show how clever he was at male psychology. 'Zeus fucked a lot too. Of course Zeus was cuckolded,' he waggled his head, 'but it didn't matter. Alex, I am the luckiest man in the world. Who else can get to go into the office in the morning and pat Aphrodite's arse?'

They all laughed, but Iannis less so. He tried to flag down Alex's attention with his hands.

'Costas lives in a house so big he has to take a taxi to get to the bedroom,' he quipped, but there was a bitterness in his joke. Iannis was a seller of black market clothes and, as Alex had witnessed herself, he had to pile his stock on his bed in the freezing winter. He was thin, very dark around the eyes, had gambler's hands, the nail beds swollen with endless nibbling, the fingertips splayed wide. His legs were crossed and his foot madly oscillated. Just as Costas thrust his paunch out into the world, Iannis sheltered his inner self in a shambling, round-shouldered walk.

Vangelis fetched the food from the kitchen, the glittering sardines swimming in the sunshine of oil and lemon, the potatoes bubbling in tomato juice. Everyone's eyes grew wide as the smell of oregano crescendoed in their nostrils. Vangelis beamed, he was at his most expansive when playing host. At work in the computer business his friends called him Zorba, which he loved.

'Shall I cut bread for you all?' Alex asked.

'No!' Costas ripped a piece off the baguette. 'In Greece we take the bread by the hand, like we take the women.'

Iannis pronged a potato with his fork. 'Very beautiful *patates*.' He spun it round in the light, amused by its chipped facets. 'Like a diamond.'

Alex laughed. 'I know, I know.'

'Can you guess who peeled them?' asked Vangelis. 'She prefers men to do the cooking.'

'She doesn't like the kitchen but she loves bars, Vangeli,' Iannis said, eyes slanted. He dipped his head, scooping in a large piece of bread dolloped with *tzatziki*.

'Before I met Alex I thought I was finished with women,' said Vangelis, taking up Alex's hand. 'But what I love about her is she leaves me alone when I have a bad mood. She's very gentle.'

She looked down at his hand, knowing how he was. He always liked to play the great love story in public. She watched him stand up and ladle out the *fassolatha*, wide-elbowed with generosity.

'*Allez, attaque!*' he announced to the table.

After they had finished eating, Vangelis whispered into Alex's ear, 'Can you make coffee?'

'What are you two saying?' Iannis leapt in. 'Whiss, whiss, whiss.'

'He said, go and wait for me in bed,' Alex joked as she left the room. She put on the coffee, taking great care to replace the jar in the exact same spot on the shelf. She thought about doing some of the dishes but they were so oily she decided to wait. Instead she stood there, just listening to the strong coffee geysering away.

Vangelis wasn't happy with the coffee.

'It's gritty. Did some of the grains go into the water?'

'No.' She blushed self-consciously in front of the others.

'Well, hey, Alex, it's not good.' He'd raised his voice.

'Well, hey, Vangeli, if you're not happy, you know what to do.'

'Aw, let him go ay, ay, ay,' said Costas with a dismissive wave of his hand. He met her eyes with something like understanding and she relaxed. Oh, sure she wasn't easy to live with either. If Vangelis was picky, she in turn was too quick to react.

'Yes, well,' Vangelis said, lowering his hackles. 'I am training you so one day you can get a husband.'

'In exchange for English lessons,' she smiled.

'The best way to learn a language is two heads on one pillow,' Costas said playfully.

'I was thinking. My first wife was dark, my ex-girlfriend was blonde, Alex is red-haired. I wonder what I will get next?'

'A slap in the face,' Alex told him and Vangelis laughed.

She kept looking at him. He held himself a little straighter, his eyes glinted, he truly came alive when he was insulting her. From a detached standpoint, she could be amused by the role-playing in front of his friends of the *kamaki,* the lover-boy. Yet it disturbed her that she desired him more when he was like this.

It was nearly one in the morning when the guests stood up to go, finally getting the hints from Vangelis' yawns.

'Tomorrow is Friday,' Iannis said, as he was about to leave. 'Shall we all go to a bar?'

'What do you think, Alex?' asked Vangelis.

She lowered her eyes. Of course she wanted to go but she knew he didn't like bars.

'*Ela more,* can't you let her tell me herself?' Iannis tried to slap Vangelis on the head. 'She doesn't have to go through you.'

'Yes, but Alex knows I'm the boss,' he said with a shrug. 'Anyway, I am the boss of you all.' He flicked his hands together to say that he was done with the matter, then grinned to show it was all a joke.

'A real boss never has to say he's the boss,' Alex said, catching Costas' eye.

'So, is it agreed we're all going out tomorrow?' asked Iannis, kissing Alex goodbye.

'I'd love to,' said Alex.

After a pause Vangelis nodded. 'Yes, but call us to make sure.'

Back in the apartment, Vangelis' brows had slumped with tiredness.

'I have worked hard tonight and you did little to help me,' he said. 'I do nothing now.' He threw an unwashed dish across the table and it clattered against the others. He stood, observing her, his lips going bloodless. She thought she could detect the small pulse ticking away in his eyelid and she knew to say nothing. 'I am going to bed,' he said.

She put more plates in the sink, listening to him in the living room, cracking the chairs together as he flung them back in place. '*Bordel*,' he muttered. '*Baraque de merde*.' He was sometimes like this after his friends came round. Even though he knew his friends were jealous that he had a foreign woman they all lusted after, she embarrassed him; she didn't play her wifely role. She shivered as she thought of climbing into bed with him, the sheets cold, keeping her distance. In this open living space there was no chance of escape.

Alex unlocked the door. She was tired from the journey back from teaching English in town. It felt cool in the apartment because it took until evening for the sun to wheel round. The pale blue walls of the living room gave the air an added freshness. The grass outside had turned tawny from the July heat, the roses were starting to peel off like grey-edged sticking plasters.

She wished she'd popped over to the bar where the English teachers hung out. A drink would have relaxed her. It was five o'clock. He would be home soon and with luck his mood would be gone. His black mood was like a wall. Nothing would work, not shouting at him, nor wheedling nor kindnesses. He was a mass of contradictions; at one moment he could seem like a hysterical woman and a macho man; the next like a spoilt brat and an aged grump. She often wondered if it was to do with the rhythms of a Mediterranean climate where brilliant sunshine would eventually turn to oppressive thunder. Her own moods were mainly temperate with sudden squalls that never lasted.

She went to the kitchen and refilled the bottle from the huge drum of Cretan olive oil, then began the nightly ritual of slicing tomato and cucumber. She imagined him happy, smiling, getting out of the car in his new red jacket, the sun warming his face and eyes. 'More colour, more colour, baby,' he always said to her, shaking his head at her drab clothes.

She was still sitting there when the car pulled in. His face wasn't good. Well, fuck you, you bastard, fuck you. She longed to do something, to smack him in the head, to run around inside it, creating havoc, kicking it all in, painting the darkness in the bright colours he so loved. No, be calm, she told herself, calm. His crisply ironed pink shirt flapped in the hot breeze as he walked towards the building.

'Hello,' he said morosely and went straight to the living room. Notes from the guitar disrupted the silence. He was a beginner, played the same riffs over and over. One night after he had played for hours, she'd set the guitar beside him in bed.

'Since you love it so much, why don't you sleep with it? See, it's even pear-shaped like a woman.' She had thought he might hit her, confusion thrumming in his face, but he had forced a laugh.

In the early days, it had been an obsession of Alex's to find out why he'd split up with his wife. 'I don't know,' he shrugged. 'I came back after work and there were napkins on the chair. I threw them off and she went mad because of these stupid napkins, then she stopped speaking, so I moved out.' After living with him for some months, Alex knew exactly what had happened.

Later, he joined her in the kitchen and dished out the cold leftovers from the previous night. Soaked in the oils, the potatoes tasted even better. Vangelis' jaw began to relax as he chewed. He ate noisily, as always. 'We must eat as we like and not care,' was one of his maxims. He mentioned his day at work briefly but mostly they sat in silence. He peeled two oranges and she watched as his hands took on a sparkly glint from contact with the greenish pith. He handed her one and she parted the segments, seeing it open up like a flower. He pulled at the segments of his own with his teeth and slurped, the juice pouring through his hand onto the marble-topped table.

'I like oranges,' he said abruptly. 'They're soft—like a woman.'

He rose from the table, stretching and yawning as if trying to take in the air of the whole world. She had seen him undergo this gradual relaxation, this softening, many times after a meal. Love came from the stomach, they said in Greece. He made coffee and they both went next door.

'My mood is almost gone,' he said as he moved in close beside her on the sofa. 'Are you okay?'

'Yes.'

He took her hand up in his and stroked her fingers. 'After all, one must profit a little when things are good.'

He pulled the shutter down at the French windows and undressed. Some sunlight still entered slit-eyed through the half-closed blind in the alcove. She watched him, loving the seam of dark hair running up through his belly button where it merged into the hairs of his chest, loving the bumpy pores of his neck. As he moved, the candle-flame muscles flickered in and out on his bulky upper arms. Half-man, half-animal, she thought with desire. My little minotaur. He was so at ease with his own body, so unabashed. He was happy to dance round the room like a Greek satyr. 'We will enjoy sex more if we laugh,' he'd said the first time.

He sat down again beside her, his finger circling her palm, mapping out a tenderness within.

'Are you thinking again?'

'Yes.'

He tutted. 'Don't think.'

'Yes, boss.'

'I'm not your boss.' There was hurt in his green eyes.

She reached out to him and soon she forgot, forgot about all that stupid trouble.

'Lucie will be a beautiful woman some day,' Vangelis said, satisfied.

He and Alex were standing in the park watching his two children play. Lucie at six had black hair with pale skin and arrestingly large blue eyes whereas her older sister, Flora, had skin the colour of toasted wheat and green eyes. Though Lucie was lauded as the beauty, Alex preferred Flora's looks; they reminded her of Vangelis.

Suddenly Vangelis dashed forward onto the grass and began chasing his children. He caught them both and started rolling them around and tickling them in a game he called 'spaghetti'. Alex noticed how the muscles swelled across his shoulders, making his white shirt almost burst at the seams, creases fanning out down the sides of his body like feathers. Then he stood up, folds of laughter still in his face, and walked back to Alex, brushing the blades of grass from his jeans.

'It worries me sometimes that Flora is too serious,' he confided.

'Oh, I don't think she is.'

'Can't you see how quiet she is? How will she get a man if she doesn't know how to play? The reason I play with my children is because playing is like making love. Do you think when Flora reaches twenty and falls in love, the man will love her because she can read well?'

She hesitated, unsure if it was a criticism of her own book-reading, and he tilted his head to the side as if to say he had won an unexpected victory. Shielding her eyes from the sun, she moved into the shade. The gravel paths were as white as sunrays and almost blinded her. For a second everything went blue and there was a buzz in her brain followed by dizziness.

'Hey, earthworm,' teased Vangelis. 'Why don't you come out into the sun?' He threw his head up and basked in it joyously. It was ninety-plus degrees and they had just come out of the small city zoo where they'd seen scrawny lions lying exhaustedly on wooden bunks, vainly trying to stir up the air with their tails.

'Lucie, Flora, let's go,' Vangelis shouted. 'Alex has had enough sun for one day.'

They walked back to the car through the Arab quarter. She loved it when they went to the Arab market, wandering past the open bags of saffron, cumin, the jars of lentils like dyed beads, the red chilli peppers and stoned olives swimming in briny buckets in a mad colour-burst.

Vangelis drove as he always did, straight and fast, too close to the car in front. They swung past the pilastered magnificence of Place Stanislas. A homeless man was sleeping on one of the benches, his bald head protruding from the neck of his coat like a stump.

'Pah, beggars,' said Vangelis in disgust. 'They come to France from the east.'

'Are you from the east, An-An?' Lucie wanted to know.

'No, the north. And west.'

'An-An, does your mother think her daughter is dead?'

Alex and Vangelis met the question with laughter.

'No, no, Lucie, she knows I'm in France,' Alex said. 'I speak to her every week on the phone.'

Dead, she thought. Now she considered it, leaving her country had been nothing compared to leaving her family. When she'd phoned to tell them she wasn't coming back at Christmas, her mother had asked, 'Are you in love with this man?' Alex had broken down in sobs and admitted she was. She'd been away so long now, she began to wonder if she'd ever belong back home.

Later, when they were alone in the apartment, it seemed unbearably empty. The lowering sun was nosing its way through the kitchen window. Within the sky was one low cloud, spindles of light shooting down like oars on a great boat, lending a vividness to everything. Chopped logs in a field had turned to the colour of split sweet potatoes.

'Oh, I wanted to say to you...' Vangelis spoke casually, almost off-handedly. 'Yesterday there was a message from the school on the answer machine. Something about leaving back books.'

'Oh.'

'So, can you tell me what it's about?' There was that strange lightness in his voice.

'I quit.'

She had quit on Thursday, in fury at Vangelis, had told her boss she was leaving France. Earlier that day she'd heard Vangelis on the phone to Iannis, saying that it was Alex's fault he hadn't had time to meet him. 'It is always Alex's fault,' he'd said, raising his voice purposely. She'd phoned the school out of rashness, she hadn't even thought of booking her journey home. Now she wasn't even sure that she had done the right thing.

'Well, I guessed that much,' he said, 'but I thought you quite liked the job.'

She could hardly look at him. She knew he was enjoying stringing out the questions, making her suffer. 'Just.'

'Just?' He imitated her shrug.

'You know I was never that into teaching.'

'But it's good money.'

'Alright then, I am tired of colonising the world with my superior language.'

'Okay. You are a free woman. It's your decision.'

'Yes, it is. But the truth is I... I was thinking about leaving.'

'I knew it. I'm not stupid.' His own eyes were bright. An awkward smile was on his face.

'What do you think?'

The smile didn't move a millimetre. 'If you're not happy...'

'We're different, you and I. I told you I wanted to travel to other places. I don't think it would work here.' She stopped suddenly. 'Why are you laughing?'

'I'm not.'

Then she saw it wasn't laughter. He was sobbing in great breaths, he was sucking at the air, his lips stretched wide in grief, his green eyes waterlogged, sinking.

'You've been thinking too much,' he cried out. 'I told you not to think.'

'Oh, God,' she heard herself say, her eyes stinging. She held out her hand to him.

Vangelis clutched at it blindly. 'When will you go?'

'I don't know.'

'Well. Well, well.'

'I'm so sorry.'

After a while, he drew back and rubbed his eyes. 'Enough, yeah?' He was in control again, the pinkiness that had invaded his tanned skin now suppressed. He reached out to gently touch her cheek, wiping it dry with his thumb. 'Will you come next door with me?'

In the living room Vangelis rubbed her hand between his as they sat on the sofa. 'After all, one must profit a little while we have the chance,' he said softly.

She put her hand across Vangelis' brow, smoothed back his hair, a swell of wrinkles on his forehead, silver flecking his hair like white caps on a black sea. His body no longer felt like it belonged to her. There was no meaning in why they had ever got together but it was better, wasn't it, than letting the body fade and wither away without a flicker of passion?

'Remember how we were at the beginning?' Alex said. 'Longing for each other, but not daring to ask?'

Vangelis looked into her face, his pupils moving restlessly as though searching for someone, trying to pinpoint her in a vast crowd.

'Don't be sad,' he said. 'When I'm retired I will go back to my family house in Crete. You can find me there. It has a big garden and we don't need money. We can live off watermelon and peaches. In Crete, the watermelons are so big, sometimes Greeks don't know whether to take them or a woman.' He nuzzled into her shoulder making her laugh to mask the seriousness of the conversation.

A few days later, ready to start the journey to the north west, Alex had a last look around the apartment. It scarcely looked any different without her. Only the bathroom was less cluttered. It occurred to her that all along she'd been living there as though it was a hotel. The bed so neatly made-up it could have been ready for a fresh guest. She stood transfixed, reflecting how one day your whole life stretched out in one country and the next it was over. It was strange how they had both cooled in the scorching heat of summer. Vangelis started the car outside, hinting for her to hurry up. She closed the front door.

The wind was already warm, flicking up little darts of ochreous dust around her feet.

'Allez, au bus!' Vangelis said, trying to muster enthusiasm, as she got in.

'I mustn't go away with your keys,' she said, passing them to him. Vangelis stared at them for a moment in her hand before accepting them. She wasn't sure what she felt. Was it relief? Was it loss? Or emptiness? Whatever it was, it was huge.

The engine thrummed below her thoughts. The morning paper had forecast gentle rain in her homeland, but in the bright sunshine she could barely fathom the notion of clouds. Nothing seemed real, her mind was still a bundle of images of her life with Vangelis, ramdom colours that were now passing into nothingness.

The bus was already waiting in the depot. Vangelis struggled along with her case, eight months of living crammed into it, heavy with parting gifts of Cretan oil, tins of halva and jars of olives.

She turned to him at the gate. 'So, this is it.'

'Yes. But I meant what I said.' He took her hand. 'If you're alone in some years, come and look for me in Crete. Angelidakis. Everyone in Crete knows our name.'

Vangelis Angelidakis. She still loved the sound of it. Angel Angel. A last kiss brushed her face, the last fleeting touch of skin, and the bus doors opened.

THE LOUGH

Damian didn't have a routine in the morning except that he got up when he woke up. This morning was different and Gráinne's voice had hooked him out of the thick sediment of dreams. He'd come round with a gasp of reluctance followed by a vigorous wriggle akin to that of a landed fish. He was still feeling groggy now as he sat tucking into his fried egg and toast.

'You'll need a good plateful if you're off to Newry,' Gráinne advised him.

If she'd been fit, she'd have cooked him the full works. 'No woman, no fry,' he thought to himself ruefully, quoting the boys down the pub.

Gráinne was sitting in her dressing gown, the bad leg up on a chair. The leg was knit into a steel brace, the wire scaffolded into the flesh, though he tried not to look at it at close quarters. Her 'bionic leg', they joked when she was in good form. This morning she was upset, wrapping the dressing gown tightly around her, as though against the chill of impending troubles.

'You'll have to speak to him,' she was urging. 'It'll have to come from you.'

'When I come back. I'm not waking him up now...'

'I wasn't saying to wake him up!' she bit back. 'He'd be like a bear with a sore head. I bloody know that, you fool. I meant later.'

He couldn't help be irritated by her, that sullen mouth. He couldn't bear to look her in the eyes these days. Oh, she'd done a great job, sure enough, bringing up Seán when he was away those years. 'Her goodness would take her to heaven,' his mother always said of her.

'We'll have to knock that sort of craic right on the head. I can't live through more of the like of that...' Her voice tailed away into the burrow of its own resentment.

'Look, I said I'll deal with it.' He took a last gulp of tea and stood up. The drawing up of his body was meant to draw a line under the conversation but there was more to come.

'It's your turn now, Damian. I've done my bit...' Better let her go on. She'd get it out of her system. Just weather it through. He kept staring at that line down her forehead, a line of concentration, not of anger, but she should never have let it grow so deep. It gave him almost a malicious satisfaction and then suddenly a rush of pity and love replaced it.

'...three years me and Seán on our tod here,' she was saying. 'I've made my sacrifice.'

He looked away, effectively shamed by the word. 'I know, I know.' He mumbled the words as if in bowed prayer to a priest's accusation of sin and edged towards the door. 'I'd better be heading on.'

She was getting up on her crutches and he gestured for her to stay.

'No, no, you sit down. I'll see myself out.'

'You want me to flipping well rust over, sitting here all day?'

'No, just...'

She paused, struggling to overcome her own crispness. 'I'll come and see you off. There was a wee taste of rain there earlier but it's cleared up now.'

At the front door, she raised her face to him for a kiss. 'Best of luck, love.' In Irish, she told him a proverb, 'Listen to the sound of the water and you will get a fish,' and he laughed. She was waving from the door as the car started. He pulled out of the drive to a further wave and was born away on the stream of traffic, knowing she would be standing there waving till the car went out of sight, as she always did. He sometimes wondered if it was due to her mother dying so young, if it had emanated from a fear of loss and was almost a propitiation to the gods.

His mind turned back to Seán. Madness! Dragged out of the pub for shouting 'Up the Ra!' during 'Roddy McCorley'. Jesus, on a Thursday night shindig when the pub was packed to the rafters. Gráinne's sister had called that morning to tell them the *scéal*, no doubt taking a malicious pleasure in it all. She'd always been jealous of them. She liked to snipe at how the ex-IRA seemed very successful in life.

He was concerned himself but, sure, the boy had been blootered. Only eighteen. At heart he was no wee rip, he was a diamond, no real badness there. He'd wanted to tell Gráinne that she was magnifying it all out of proportion. It was because she was trapped at home most days. He knew how it was having spent three years in Long Kesh.

The West Link was heaving with rush hour traffic within its ugly concrete walls. The road was no more than a deep trench, purpose-built in the seventies to cut off the troublesome West of the city from the centre. Above the grey wall, he could see the roof of the Orange Hall and the King Billy statue with its sword pointed high, seemingly stuck into a white cloud like a breadknife into a loaf. He was never normally out on the roads this hour of the morning. He taught Irish in the afternoons and worked on the committee of organisations like Families for Peace and the Free Palestine Campaign but, until Gráinne's accident, he hadn't contemplated teaching full time. Three months without her own teaching wage had struck them hard, especially with Seán's university fees to be paid, and it would be a couple of months before the metal brace was off. He checked his watch. He was in good time for the interview.

The low September sun flashed into the car through gaps in the jagged hedgerows of hawthorn, ash and elderberry. Mallow and convolvulus still managed to bloom from the strangling maturation. Memories flitted into his head as they always did when he travelled, as though the motion forward pre-empted a journey into the past. He remembered being told by his mother that as a toddler he ate the tops of flowers while his brother had a taste for sand and gravel. It struck him as ironic. Flower-eater, he laughed at himself. Hippy child, yet his brother who'd liked grit had never had the same appetite for war.

He passed through a village, the road now lined with pebble-dashed houses. The flags and Union Jack bunting hung limply like a thousand red rags to a bull, but he tried to quell the loathing they engendered because it wasn't worth it. He didn't believe in the armed struggle any more. All along he had regarded it as a tactic, not an historical imperative and the problem with war was that you couldn't hear the arguments above the sound of the bullets. Enculturation was the way forward. He would tell that to the principal. He liked cross-community classes best. The likes of that loyalist hard nut who came in and said, 'I want to learn about Coochoolin and how he bate them Fenian bastards.' He and Gráinne had had a great old laugh about it. 'Ah well, you have to start somewhere,' he'd shrugged. 'From tiny seeds...'

'Sprout amusing chestnuts,' she had finished. He'd always appreciated Gráinne's sense of humour, oh, that was one thing that had stayed the same alright.

Man, but the country was looking well. Change the subject, change the subject, his mind told himself frantically as a heat spread like flames over his body. It didn't do any good thinking about the past.

His mobile phone was ringing.

'Hello?'

'Hello, love. Still on the road?'

Twenty years of marriage had made him a tracker of every nuance, each cracked twig of meaning. 'What's wrong, Gráinne?'

'Just had a call from the principal's secretary. He rang in sick this morning.'

'But I'm nearly there now.'

'I know, don't I? She's not off the phone five seconds. I told her what were they playing at, calling at this time? And he was the one who'd come begging for your expertise.'

The voice leapt up at the end of every sentence in indignation. That was her. Patriotic, familial, quick to rise. Perhaps it was only for her that he had joined. 'We can't all be fireside generals,' she had retorted to her relatives at the time.

'Well, that's that.' He didn't know what to say. The truth was he didn't really care about setting up more classes. Certainly they needed the money but he was no longer the Irish language activist he'd once been. The trouble was he didn't want her to know that, didn't want to speak loosely and incriminate himself. *Incriminate?* That wasn't the right word but was it really true that his wife had taken the place of the authorities, observing and distrusting him? 'I'll look on the bright side. Good to get out and about anyway.'

'I dare say. All right for some.' Her voice was smaller. He hadn't meant to remind her.

He was on the look-out for a place to turn when the car some way ahead of him put on its brake lights. His breath caught in his throat. Two men carrying AK-47s were blocking the road and a third was approaching the driver's window. They were masked, faceless. What the hell was going on? A hijack?

After a brief questioning the driver in front was signalled on with a jerk of the gun barrel and the car sped off again.

Damian crawled forward. His side window buzzed down.

'This is the Irish Republican Army. Do you understand?' the man barked.

Shit! He recognised the voice. It had to be McCartan. The nose emerged broadly from the opening in the balaclava and it shone red in the sun, the black pores like strawberry pips. The brown eyes patrolled Damian's face aggressively.

'I understand,' said Damian who was torn between defiance and nonchalance and failed to convey anything.

'Let's see your driving licence.'

Damian didn't make a move. *He knows who I am and he's making a cunt of me.*

One of the two men blocking the road, the butt of the AK resting on an angular hip, shouted across, 'Let him go on.' He and his comrade backed out of Damian's way onto the verge.

Damian revved wildly to show he despised his inquisitor and drove off. He checked them in his mirror, trying to make sense of what had just happened.

The only thing he hit on was the recent trouble over a roadside memorial to seven Protestant workmen ambushed and gunned down in the seventies. This was a Republican area and the people didn't want it. The Real IRA never wasted a chance to show roadside muscle.

Anthony Paul McCartan. Dissident Republican, hated peace. Fuck your doves, he'd shouted. Bad bastard. 'A man of many talons,' Gráinne had once said about McCartan. He thought about picking up the phone but decided it would keep. It was a bit of excitement to tell Gráinne but he wished now he'd said something to McCartan. She would have admired that.

His mind was flying and instead of turning for home, he took a left towards the Mournes that were lying blue in the distance. When would they ever catch on that the armed struggle was over? Oh, he was upset now. And it was too late to push the memories back down.

In Long Kesh, Damian's cleverness and the fact that he was well liked had gained him the position of information officer. He was the first to speak to the new arrivals and write down what they had told their police interrogators. This way the Officer Commanding could establish whether evidence came from the prisoners or from the street. At first Damian didn't mind the work but it began to scare him how much he knew about operations and, what was worse, about individuals.

After his release, he'd wanted out, but O'Neill who'd been made head of the Internal Security Unit begged him to help out with intelligence just one last time. He needed a hand with a family of informers, a single mother to be exact, with three teenagers, name of McLaughlin. The four had reputations for thieving in the area though surprise, surprise—they had few criminal convictions. Go figure, O'Neill mimicked in that New York wiseguy way you'd hear on TV cop shows...

Ah, he hadn't thought about it in a long while. The main thing was, he was alive and it was a fine old day and the road kept lifting and plunging, dealing out views over the trelliswork of arched brambles. Autumn was starting to infiltrate the green with bromines, prunes and reds. The mountains were looming closer, the colours separating into stoles of red fern and bell heather. He could make out the tor of Bearnagh and the Saddle. He hadn't been near the Mournes since the accident.

It hadn't been such a deep hollow between the rocks but it was the way Gráinne had fallen. He'd pulled her out screaming from the pain in her leg and now she lay on the heather bed, her hands pressing against the sides of her temples, her bent elbows two harsh peaks against the sky.

Thankfully Damian had brought the mobile with him. He had automatically asked for a helicopter from the Republic. No, he didn't want one from Ballykinlar army base even though it took only fifteen minutes. He didn't need help from the British Army and never would.

'It'll not be that long, I'm sure, love,' he said, looking to the southern skies.

She nodded, quiet, the pain rumpling her eyes.

Half an hour passed. 'All right, I'll phone for Ballykinlar,' he decided.

Her ferocity shocked him. 'Don't even think about it,' she hissed.

He came too close and she put her arms across her leg as an angry vixen would protect her cub.

Hours later, they told him at the hospital that the leg had swollen up so much from the shattering it had hampered their operation. She would be left with a permanent limp. It had been the beginning of the guilt. The problem was he kept seeing a dull hurt in her eyes and he suspected it was from that moment on the Saddle when he'd changed his mind, calling into question the decision that had left her crippled. It was as though he had relegated all the years she'd suffered, bringing up Seán alone, into the realm of stupid, posturing ideals.

Yet, it wasn't only the accident that had left him questioning his principles. The disappearance of Donna McLaughlin had recently returned to make front page news, backed by photos of JCBs digging on the wrong strip of shoreline, but nevertheless too close for comfort. Who could have told? Not one of them there that night, yet the smallest piece of information no bigger than the grain of sand on a shovel could herald an investigation. He'd sought out McGhie who dismissed it all. The police, he said, didn't have a baldy, they couldn't even find a body in a morgue; they were just back to their old tricks of trying to shame the IRA. Damian found it hard to have a serious conversation with McGhie these days. He was always in the bars, smoking dope and popping pills, raking around with a much younger crowd.

A long time ago he had told Gráinne about the night at Carlingford Lough. Yes, there had been a time he had been able to confide in her. But it was strange how all the years of memories had melted away into two defining, antipodal points: the first declaration of her love twenty years before and the declaration of hatred. A wordless hatred on that day in the mountains, a silence eventually filled by the whirring blades of the helicopter.

He found himself thinking about Seán, scarcely able to visualise the boy as he was a mere sketch of the man to come, the reddish hair jutting out on his chin as if to enhance his unfinished face, still famished from the unfulfilled desire to live the same exciting life as his father. Damian shivered for Seán's future. Oh, it was easy for the boy to 'sleep on another man's wounds', easy to support a cause he hadn't suffered for, to shout about the IRA when he had no idea of the truth.

He checked his own reflection in the mirror. Red and silver-haired and stronger jawed than his son. Yet there was a clapped-in hollowness under the eyes and cheekbones and under the chin and it scared him a little. It made him think of subsidence, panicked him, and yet it was nothing more than the ageing process.

He changed gear, realising now that the only thing he had a grip on was the car. He was going round the back of the mountains without sparing them a second glance. He needed to return to the spot. It was a compulsion. After eight years it had fought its way out of his head.

He rounded the bend and suddenly was met by the blue of the curved inlet, pearly-rimmed with waves like the inside of a mussel shell. It was a long way down and the road began to plunge steeply. A poem kept repeating itself, unpeeling its pithy bitterness into his mind, 'Man to the hills, woman to the shore.'

He parked the car at the side of the coast road. From there he followed a lane with its centre of yellow grass exploding out of the tarmac like a long line of lit gunpowder. His view was partially obscured by low clumps of buckthorn and gorse but he took a well-trodden path which meandered down to the stony edge of the shore. There, the sun on the sea dazzled him. Reefs of brown rock purpled under the ebbing blue like a bed of heather. The green hills of the Republic rose peacefully from the far side of the shore. So beautiful and suddenly he couldn't understand how anyone could destroy their own memory of the place. It was O'Neill who'd decided on the 'beach job' over the Monaghan bogland that McGhie had advocated. O'Neill had known the lough like the back of his hand from childhood summers, not like the rest of them who annually trekked up to Donegal.

The tide, on the ebb, was disappearing fast over the mudflats, leaving great arched tidal pools. The oystercatchers and waders were busily feeding. Gulls sat on the warm sand, their heads nesting over their bodies like whorled shells.

He looked for points of reference. It hadn't been pitch black that night and the hunter's moon had shone on the algae bubbling in the water. Initially, they had thought the natural light too bright but there'd been safety in a wind that had smothered the sound of their digging in the creaks of buckthorn and the whistles through the air-stops in boulders. Bitter cold it had been. McGhie had shone the torch across to a wall, a tumble-down affair, gnawed away by high winter tides, and O'Neill had gone ballistic. 'You want to show half the country we're here?' he'd raged but now Damian thought about it O'Neill had wanted to conceal it as much from them as from the eyes of the world. He had led them blindly through a long, circuitous route of scratching gorse to an exact spot he had intended never to be retraced.

There was a wall to Damian's left and fences to the other side. The wall, recently rebuilt, demarcated a row of neat, renovated holiday cottages. The peace process had transformed this whole stretch of coastline. All the wildness that had protected the fighters was going out of this land and there was no going back, he thanked God.

Scanning the sands, he caught sight of the bright trail of water from a tractor parked by oyster beds. Beside the tractor he could just make out the silhouette of a small, bent figure with a shovel. His own heart seemed too fast now, out of synch with the slow pulse in the blue water.

He stepped down onto the jingling shingle and shale that slid uncomfortably under his smooth soles. A line of dry debris and foam marked the height of that morning's tide. He picked his way across to the wall.

There was no proof whatsoever that out of the few miles of shoreline, he'd chanced on the place but it was the rounded turn of the wall that convinced him he was right. Not ten yards away was the hump of spiky marram grass exposing a sandy soil underneath. He walked on over the uneven surface, the clink of broken things seemingly chained to his feet. In front lay a tree washed up by a storm. He reached out for its branch and steadied himself. The sea had stripped the bark, bleached the wood and antlered its branches, bowling out eyes where roots had been, sculpting it into a mythical beast. He looked up at the hump of sand and saw something that chilled his blood.

'Mammy, mammy,' her children had cried as they'd taken her. No resistance. Hot, muffle-headed in balaclavas. People from the top floors of the flats cheered. 'Scum, scum, scum!' Putting the duct tape across her mouth. Standing outside the cowshed near Newry, the taste of cigarette in the mouth, cold of grass worming in between the toes, while O'Neill interrogated. Then the shot. Racing in the door. The fucker had done it. In the back of her head.

He suddenly found he was sobbing. It wasn't bone he'd seen. It was the blanched root of the driftwood. Gráinne, Gráinne. All those years protecting Seán, pretending to him that his Dad was a hero. He could only guess at the dead woman, imagine that perhaps she'd cooperated with the police to protect her children. Maybe she was innocent. It made sense that O'Neill had killed her to cover up his own leaked information.

He wiped his eyes, remembering the tricolour-draped funerals of fallen comrades and the mantra:

Life springs from death; and from the graves of patriot men and women spring living nations.

He felt sick. A singing went through his head. The waste! The lies and the bullshit they fed you. Out of graves nothing springs but grass!

He turned away and cast his eyes out to the flats and sea,

encircling all in the net of his vision. A slender heron suddenly spread out great clumsy wings as though struggling into a heavy winter coat. Then the horror returned as his memory again rewrote the view with the black ink of that night. His head whipped to the side, alert to the sound of a man crunching along the beach towards him. He watched every step. The man knew, *he knew*. He was heading straight to confront him.

The man had wind-eddied hair under a small wool hat. He looked like he belonged to this beach. Yes, this was a man who knew every lie of sand and rock, his long legs striding along, his broad torso bobbing like a pounding heart.

'Grand weather we're having,' he shouted across, directing with due economy the tilt of his smile onto the side facing Damian. As he passed by, Damian nodded back, air runnelling out of his lungs in relief.

He began to walk away himself quickly, his shoes turning and slipping on the stones. Dried bladderwrack split and fire-cracked under his step. The racket was too much, as if he was larger than life, as if he was sounding an alarm. He stopped abruptly. Some of the noise was coming from overhead. The low, hacking throb. He could see the tiny black fly dance and hover, thinking, plotting in the blue sky.

Oh, my God! He made a dash for it, legs sliding apart, the beach opening up treacherously beneath him. It came back into his head, the man in the balaclava standing in the road who let him go on, his voice, the tough guy stance... O'Neill, he'd never gone away, was still watching him. *I'll jab you in the head if you ever tell.* He glanced over his shoulder, nearly falling. Up there, they were following him! Gráinne, he cried. Where was she when he needed her? The blades of the helicopter whirred ever louder, the shadow buzzed across the mudflats, zipping, swooping, feeding on its expanse and he ran on, tortured, bent over, his hands clutched to his ears.

ACKNOWLEDGEMENTS

Acknowledgements are due to the following publications in which versions of these stories first appeared: 'Revival' was published in *Verbal Arts Magazine* and 'Catholic Boy' was published in *The Stinging Fly*.

Thanks to Lisa Frank and John Walsh, and to Damian Smyth and the Arts Council of Northern Ireland who have always supported me. Also, a private thank you to the great people behind these stories.

ROSEMARY JENKINSON was born in Belfast and is an award-winning playwright and short story writer. Her plays include *The Bonefire* (winner of the 2006 Stewart Parker BBC Radio Award), *Basra Boy, White Star of the North, Planet Belfast, Here Comes the Night, Michelle and Arlene* and *Lives in Translation*. She won the 2001 Black Hill Magazine Short Story Competition, third prize in the Brian Moore Short Story Awards and was shortlisted for the 2002 Hennessy Award for New Writing. Her first collection of short stories, *Contemporary Problems Nos. 53 & 54*, was published in 2004 by Lagan Press. Her second short story collection, *Aphrodite's Kiss & Further Stories*, was published by Whittrick Press in 2016. She's won many General Arts Awards from the Arts Council of Northern Ireland and was the 2017 Artist-in-Residence at the Lyric Theatre in Belfast.